"What are you doing?" she screamed.

She ran over to him and tried to pry the album out of his hands before he could toss any more pictures into the flames. But he held onto the album as he watched the photographs curl, blacken, then disappear into ashes.

"Daddy!"

"Roger! Stop it!"

"You're burning our family pictures," Sarah yelled.

"That was our old family," he said calmly, so calmly that despite the heat rising up from the fireplace, despite the flush on her face from the flames, she was colder than she'd ever been in her entire life.

RUMORS AND WHISPERS

Marilyn Levy

FAWCETT JUNIPER • NEW YORK

A Fawcett Juniper Book
Published by Ballantine Books
Copyright © 1990 by Marilyn Levy

Library of Congress Catalog Card Number: 90-90290

ISBN 0-449-70327-4

Printed in Canada

First Edition: December 1990

Chapter One

Her hand shook as she squeezed the ochre tube. The paint oozed out like rusty toothpaste. She was always nervous for the first few minutes of class, until she settled into her work and forgot about the chaos going on all around her. It was unnerving being the only girl in the room with a bunch of guys who had signed up for art so they'd be paroled from sitting in the library for detention during this period. Some of them actually liked to paint once they got around to it, and she thought a few of them even had some talent, but most of them had no real interest in art and couldn't tell the difference between a Picasso and a Cezanne.

Actually, she hadn't had any idea she could paint either, until this semester. She'd taken art history at her old school, and her parents had sometimes taken her and her brother to the Cleveland Museum of Art before they had moved, but she hadn't really tried her hand at doing anything artistic since she'd covered the walls of her room with finger paints when she was three years old. Her mother had been so upset with her splashes of reds and blues and yellows—which Sarah thought were incredibly beautiful—that she had gathered up all of Sarah's paints and thrown them into the garbage can.

When she started nursery school, Sarah couldn't believe the teachers actually wanted her to mush her hands in the paints and "express" herself. She remembered just sitting in front of her large sheet of manila paper for a long time while all the other kids smeared theirs from corner to corner. The messier their papers got, the happier they were, but she could only allow herself to dip one finger into the yawning colorful jars of paints and carefully draw a house with four people standing in front of it, a mother, a father, a brother, and a sister.

So what was she doing in a painting class with a bunch of Cro-Magnon specimens whose mothers had obviously believed in the Jackson Pollock school of art? They seemed to have no trouble at all covering their canvases—or themselves for that matter—with iridescent welts of color that assaulted her sensibilities. She had signed up for the class for the wrong reason, just as most of them had. But her reason was very different from theirs. She had squeezed painting into her schedule, on top of four major classes, because she couldn't stand the thought of having two free periods. She was scared to have unoccupied time. Lunch was bad enough, but at least she had something to do with her hands during lunch. During third and fourth periods she had nothing to do but study and feel everyone else's eyes dart past her as they sat around talking, making plans, or throwing Frisbees in the open quadrangle between the high school buildings.

So, two weeks into the semester she had gone to the dean of students to find out what was available in that time slot. Consequently, she found herself enrolled in this art class. And even though it made her nervous, it was better than sitting on a bench in the quadrangle watching the world go by without her.

"I like that. I like that a lot, Sarah," Mr. Hill said as he leaned over to examine her painting more closely.

Sarah could feel her cheeks burn. Getting attention was almost worse than being ignored.

"This current trend toward realism in painting is gaining

popularity now. Alex Katz, Eric Fischl are both doing extremely well." He leaned over and looked at her painting more closely. "This is good, very good. You have excellent control."

"Thanks," Sarah muttered, without looking up at Mr. Hill. He was nice enough, she thought. She knew he meant well and was only trying to encourage her, but everyone else was looking over at her now and snickering. She hoped he wouldn't leave the room today like he did lots of other times when they were working. She dreaded that. Things sometimes got way out of hand when he was gone for more than five minutes. She didn't know if he had weak kidneys or what, but she couldn't imagine why he had to run out all the time. And as far as Alex Katz and the other guy he'd mentioned, she had no idea who they were. She'd never heard about them in her art history course.

But she smiled to herself, almost pleased with her good luck, for a change. She could hardly believe that this realism, or whatever it was called, was suddenly acceptable, because that was the only way she could possibly paint. She could never, never fill her canvas with circles that were lopsided and off center or squares that were irregular. She could never have pasted found objects like pieces of an old tire or fence on her precious canvas, or paint what looked like graffiti right through the center of her picture the way some of the guys did. And Mr. Hill encouraged that, too. Those ugly words painted in black that seemed to rip right through their canvases and hit you between the eyes when you looked at them.

She was relieved when Mr. Hill began to move away from her easel, but then he turned back to her and said, "The Museum of Contemporary Art has a few paintings by Eric Fischl. Have you ever been down there?"

Sarah shook her head no. Not only had she never been down there—wherever "there" was—she hadn't even been to downtown Los Angeles since they'd moved here last summer before school started. She knew it was about an hour's drive from Longacre, which had its own downtown area, but the freeways were still confusing to her, and her mother simply refused to use them at all. So she'd been to the beach, and she'd driven around Longacre, but she had never gone downtown and actually had no idea exactly where it was. Her father's office was in Westwood. She'd been there, but she knew that wasn't downtown, though it was the home of UCLA.

"I think we should arrange a field trip," Mr. Hill said as he moved on to Jimmy Moderelli's desk.

Sarah's heart sank. A field trip with this bunch of goons! They'd probably tear the museum apart. Or worse, they'd steal the tires off the bus and leave her and Mr. Hill stranded there for eternity, staring out the window of the museum like the Duane Hanson statues she had seen at an exhibit at the National Gallery in Washington last year. Everyone thought the statues were alive until they came closer and realized they only represented real people.

"Excuse me. Keep working. I'll be right back," Mr. Hill said as he headed for the door, coughing. He'd had a bad cold all week. Sarah thought he looked even more pale today than usual, however. Of course, he didn't exactly fit her picture of a tanned, robust southern Californian, anyway, with his mousy brown hair that seemed to droop over his ears looking for a resting place, his watery gray eyes, and his sallow skin. Not that he was bad looking. He wasn't really. He was kind of cute, if you liked thin guys. But he was a little too thin as far as Sarah was concerned. The guys in Youngstown, Ohio, where she had lived all her life till now, had a lot more meat on them. At least they looked like they did. During most of the school year, of course, it was hard to tell because everyone hibernated under layers of sweaters and coats. But out here in California everyone was thin. Even parents. She was beginning to get used to it. Her own mother and father had even begun to look a little doughy to her now, and she expected them to announce any minute that they had joined a health club like everyone else they'd met here.

"Know what?" Bobby Muladore asked conspiratorially, jumping up as soon as Mr. Hill left the room.

"What?" Jimmy Moderelli shouted across the room, ready to join Bobby in anything Bobby felt compelled to do at that moment.

"Okay. Okay. This is what I heard," he shrieked. "We're gonna have a live model next semester. I overheard Hill telling McAllister."

"So?" Jimmy said, obviously disappointed.

"So! What do you mean, 'so?' "

"I mean, so what? Big deal," Jimmy said, dipping his brush into cadmium red and smearing it on his canvas.

"Moderelli, you are so stupid," Bobby said disdainfully. "Don't you know anything?"

"I know lots of things."

"Then you oughta know that models in art classes are nude—as in naked, as in in the flesh, as in raw, as in what are you doing after class. You know?"

"I oughta know," Jimmy said slowly, a big grin spreading over his face and exposing a huge gap between his front teeth.

The whole class let out a shriek. "When? When?" a boy named Tom shouted.

"Next semester. I told you, next semester," Bobby said indignantly.

"Then I'm signing up for art again," Nick said, all but drooling.

Sarah lowered her head and tried to disappear into her painting. Maybe if she stood perfectly still they'd forget she was there. They never paid much attention to her anyway, except Jimmy who usually managed to make at least one stupid comment a day either about her or to her.

There was a lot of speculation about just who this nude

model was going to be and exactly what they were going to do with her after class. Sarah's face was burning, but she was determined not to look up, not to expose herself in any way.

Suddenly the room got very quiet. She kept working on her canvas. The quiet got louder. She dipped her brush into the glob of black paint on her palette and began stroking in strands of hair. Her hand shook. The quiet in the room exploded. Without looking up, she felt Bobby Muladore move over next to her. Every one of her senses went into high gear. Suddenly, she could smell the oil from the paints in front of her. She could even tell the difference between the red, the blue, and the black just by their smell. The odor was so strong, she felt like gagging. Her ears picked up every sound in the room and outside in the hallway. Someone sneezed. Another person was breathing heavily. A third cleared his throat. Feet shuffled by outside the door. Let one of them be Mr. Hill's, she pleaded silently, her eyes glued to her canvas, which began to jump out at her menacingly. The black was too black. The reds looked like blood. Why had she decided to paint the girl's dress red? She jammed her brush into the swirl of white paint on her palette, mixed it into the red, and made the dress pink—sickeningly pink. A color she hated because it wasn't a true color. It was a compromise color. She wanted to wipe it out. Forgetting her usual caution, she began to rub at the color with her finger. Then she drew back. The wet paint felt cold and slimy. She quickly wiped it off on the loose-fitting smock she wore during art class to protect her clothes. The smock had somehow managed to remain almost spotless until now.

She could feel Bobby almost breathing down her neck. No one said a word. Her back stiffened. With one deft move he unzipped the zipper running down the back of the smock and announced that he thought Sarah might make a good model, but they'd have to check out her figure first. No one could actually tell what she looked like under that sack.

Sarah could feel tears of both rage and shame begin to fill her eyes, but she refused to lose control of her emotions, so she swallowed hard and drew them back in again. She was enraged that anyone would be so crude and insensitive, but at the same time she felt humiliated because she was almost pleased that he knew her name.

She stood there frozen as Bobby's hand reached around to pull the smock from her shoulders. Suddenly, he released the material, and she felt the air around her stiffen with tension.

"Mr. Hill's coming down the hall," someone said.

Out of the corner of her eyes she saw Bobby dash back to his easel. She slid down onto her stool and began to tremble.

"Don't pay any attention to him," that same someone whispered softly.

Still shaking, Sarah looked over at a boy named David who always stayed to himself in the far corner of the classroom. Nobody seemed to pay much attention to him, including Mr. Hill. She had actually forgotten he was there. But here he was, standing next to her, quietly trying to make her feel better.

The tears she had managed to control until now came spilling out. Since she had moved to Longacre, David was the first student who had actually spoken to her as if she were a real person, not just a number in line or an object of ridicule.

Chapter Two

Lunch period was worse than usual today. She still felt very vulnerable despite those words of encouragement from David—whoever he was. She couldn't even remember exactly what he looked like. She'd never bothered to more than glance at him until this morning, and then she was too nervous and upset to really look at him. Well, hell, he was probably just another outcast like she was. Maybe he was a new student at Longacre High, too. Or worse, maybe he was the school geek. Just her luck to have someone like that on her side.

She turned the page of her social studies book though she hadn't read one word of it. Without looking up she took a bite of her sandwich, but she had a hard time swallowing it, even though she had already chewed what was in her mouth over a hundred times. She picked up her carton of milk, took a long drink, and tried to wash it down, but it seemed to stick in her throat. Or maybe something else was stuck there. Something more intangible. Something that made her shrivel up and turn away whenever anybody looked at her. She didn't know why she reacted that way. She had had lots of friends in Youngstown. Well, maybe not lots, but there had been Meg and Molly and Rob, kids she'd known all her life. Of course, she felt comfortable with them. They'd all gone to nursery school together, then kindergarten, then elementary school, then middle school, and finally high school. And then—just when everything was really looking good, just when she'd been elected president of the French Club for her senior year—her parents had laid the big one on her. They were moving.

Molly's mother had invited her to live with them for the school year so she could graduate with her class, but her parents had vetoed that right away. California was too far away from Ohio, and they couldn't—or wouldn't—leave her behind. She had begged her father to wait for one more year, but his company was expanding. They were opening corporate offices in California, and this was his big opportunity to move up.

So last June, right after her brother's graduation, they packed up everything they hadn't already sold at their house sale, and they moved out of the home she had lived in all her life. Then they said their good-byes, took a taxi to the airport, and boarded a plane for what might just as well have been Mars.

She knew California would be different from Ohio. She had expected it to be. But she hadn't expected it to be like living on another planet.

When they pulled up in the cab, she couldn't believe her eyes. The new house wasn't anything like the one they had lived in in Youngstown. Their old house had a basement, a first floor, an upstairs with three bedrooms and two bathrooms, and an attic. It was on a hill, and there was a big front yard and a big fenced in backyard where their swings, a jungle gym, and a sliding board still got some use every now and then, even though she and Doug were way too sophisticated for that kind of thing. Just for kicks, though, she sometimes liked to push off and see how high she could go with her eyes shut.

But this house was so tacky. She couldn't believe her mother and father had spent a week looking and had come up with this. It looked like a garage—and it was about the

same size as one, too. She thought her parents had wrenched
her out of the place where she really belonged because her
father had gotten a big promotion. But this—this looked
like a demotion to her.

She glanced over at Doug. He rolled his eyes up into his
head and shrugged his shoulders, though he wasn't quite as
unhappy about leaving Ohio as she was and didn't seem to
care where they lived. After all, he had gotten to finish
school there. Actually, he had barely made it. Doug was not
exactly National Merit Scholarship material. In fact, he was
what they euphemistically referred to at Rayan High, a fifth-
year senior, and for a while they had all been just a little
nervous about his even making it at all. At the beginning of
June, he still owed two English papers. The last day of
school he finally turned them in, and he was allowed to
walk down the aisle at graduation. He was going to Longacre Junior College now, and their parents were hoping he'd
"find himself."

Sarah sighed. They were always so worried about Doug.
She could hear them whispering at night about how he was
ruining his life because he wouldn't study. While he was
still in high school, they took away his car. They took away
his records. They took away his tape deck. They took away
anything they could take, but nothing changed. Doug still
skipped classes and still refused to do his work. Her parents
thought he was insolent and stubborn. They were exasperated with the way he performed, but Sarah had a feeling that
her brother refused to do his work, not because he didn't
want to do it, but because he couldn't do it. He could do his
math homework just fine. In fact, he usually got *A*'s in
math, but she knew he couldn't read very well, that even
simple words confused him. Once he was trying to read his
social studies assignment out loud. He thought no one was
listening, but Sarah had heard him say, "the Untied States
of America." At first she thought he was kidding around.

The separate states did seem untied to her when she thought about it, especially now that she was living in one of them that seemed to have no connection whatsoever to the state she had lived in before. She realized when he went on, however, that he wasn't fooling around. He was struggling to read the material.

She had tried to talk to her parents about it, but they had refused to listen. She had tried to talk to Doug about it, but he got so defensive and angry that she had just dropped it.

He was taking an art class and a computer programming course at the junior college now, not exactly what her parents considered appropriate, but he seemed pretty happy about it. Maybe he would find himself here. She hoped so, but as for her, Sarah had no such illusions about herself. She was lost—totally, totally lost here. The best she could hope for was the strength to keep it together until graduation. Then she'd head back to Ohio, and she'd go to Ohio State with her friends—if she could make it through this horrendous year.

It had been bad from the first day they got to California. From the moment she saw the house. And the inside wasn't any better than the outside. Sure, she had her own room, but it was half the size of her room in Youngstown. And there was no family room or dining room in this house. It was just a box with a living room, a dining area, three bedrooms, and two bathrooms. It amazed her that her parents actually seemed proud of having bought this white stucco oversized box, and it amazed her even more when she learned that it had cost three times more than their "real" house.

There was no place to go in the new house. They were always on top of each other. But she had to admit her mother was right about one thing—it was easy to take care of. No running up and down the stairs to do laundry, no endless vacuuming, no long hours cutting the grass. Everything could be done in half a day.

Only once they were settled, once they had begun to get used to the place, once she had acknowledged California did have its good points, like the greatest weather in the world, they all realized something was missing. Something very important. Other people. Not one of their neighbors had come to welcome them into the neighborhood. No one had brought them homemade cookies, or had baked a cake for them, or had invited them to come over for homemade ice cream. No one had rung their bell and asked them to join the local Republican party—or even the Democrats, for that matter. No one had run over, delighted there was someone of baby-sitting age who had moved in. No one called and asked her mother over for coffee. No one invited her father to play golf on Saturday. They lived there for a whole week before the phone rang, and then it was only a wrong number.

Gradually, her father made some friends at work, but his office was forty minutes from their house, and most of the people he met lived in other areas even farther away than they did. So it was hard making plans to get together. Once people had fought the freeway jungles to get home, they had no desire to turn around and go out again, unless they went to their local movies or restaurants.

Her parents had finally joined the First Methodist Church in Longacre, and even though they hadn't been that big on going in Youngstown, they started attending services here. Her mother met some other women. Her father was invited to join the golf club, and they were gradually making a place for themselves in the community, but it wasn't as easy to learn how to fit in here as it was in Ohio, and you had to keep on your toes all the time because people had different expectations. The rules were different. People talked about different things. They talked about health clubs and about weight, about how much everybody's house cost and how much they thought it might go up in the next few months, things her parents had never once discussed with their best friends in Ohio, who had no idea how much they had gotten for their house when they sold it.

Because they were living on top of each other, when Sarah was in her bedroom, she could very clearly hear conversations coming from the living room and kitchen. At first it amused her to listen to all the neighborhood gossip. Then it bothered her. These people never talked about anything except themselves. She wondered if they read the paper, though occasionally they did mention something they'd seen on the eleven o'clock news.

She also had a hard time keeping all of them straight. No one seemed to be married to the father or mother of his or her children. She had had friends in Ohio whose parents were divorced. She even remembered when Molly's parents had gone through theirs. Both Molly and her mother had been totally devastated, and neither of them had really ever forgiven Molly's father for walking out on them. But these people in California were all still friendly. In fact, they were very friendly. Mrs.—call me Emily all my friends do— Collins was planning a trip to Hawaii during Christmas vacation, which sounded wonderful until she mentioned that she was going with her ex-husband and their two kids while her present husband would be vacationing in Aspen with his ex, her new husband, and their daughter.

She had met Mrs. Collins's daughter and her stepdaughter at a sushi supper given by the Collinses at the end of summer. She had even tried to talk to them, but she hadn't known what to say. Sure, they liked the same music, wore the same kinds of clothes, had similar haircuts, but they were different. They looked different. They talked differently. Wendy and Joni giggled too much and too loudly. And they obviously thought Sarah was a colossal bore.

When they saw her at school the first day of classes, they smiled, said hi, then rushed off to meet someone much more interesting.

During second period Sarah had spotted Wendy, Mrs. Collins's daughter, again and relieved that she was, at least, a familiar face, she steeled herself and walked over to ask Wendy where the Liberal Arts building was.

"Oh my god," Wendy said. "You really are out of it, aren't you?" she giggled.

"Excuse me," Sarah said, confused by her response.

"I mean, my god, you're standing right in front of it, for god's sake. There. It's right there," she said, pointing to an unmarked building directly in front of them.

"Sorry," Sarah said, feeling very stupid.

"I mean *everyone* knows that's Lib Arts," Wendy said, sucking in her cheeks, blinking her eyes vapidly, and shaking her head from side to side.

"I thought I was lost," Sarah said, "and I was afraid I'd be late to class."

"You thought you were *lost*?" Wendy asked, laughing. "On this little campus? My god, what are you going to do when you go to college? You better consider applying at schools with a student body of under five thousand," she added as she ran up the steps of Lib Arts and into the building.

Sarah followed her, but Wendy was already surrounded by a half dozen of her very best friends, so Sarah just walked past them, looking for room 202, which she figured must be on the second floor. She walked up the stairs and looked around. There were no room numbers. There was the Shakespeare Room, the Dante Room, the Gabriel García Márquez Room, the Virginia Woolf Room, the Tolstoy Room. But no room 202.

The bell rang, and a group of students jostled her as they lunged past her into the yawning jaws of Shakespeare, Dante, García Márquez, and Virginia Woolf, filling the rooms with their laughter and shouts.

Everyone knew where he or she was going except her. She was totally and completely lost and, still stinging from the response to her last question, she was afraid to ask for help.

"You must be a new student," a male teacher said, walking up to her.

Afraid to speak, she nodded her head yes.

The teacher reached for her schedule, shook his head, and smiled. "They changed the names of the rooms, but they never bothered changing the computers," he said. "Room 202 is now Dante. Right over there."

She was flooded with relief and felt incredibly grateful to this man, who at the moment seemed like the kindest person she'd ever met in her life. It wasn't until two weeks later that she walked into his art class and realized that the man was Mr. Hill, her painting teacher.

Sarah felt a sudden chill, pulled her sweater around her, and looked up from her book. The weather seemed to be changing. By this time of year in Ohio, it would be way too cold to even consider sitting outside. It was almost the middle of November. Molly and Meg and Rob would be preparing for the first big snow. They'd have gone to at least one French Club meeting, and they'd be hoarse from yelling and screaming at Friday night football games. Everyone at Rayan went to the games, and no one could ever talk on Monday mornings. She didn't know if the kids at Longacre went to games or not. If they did, they went without her. She certainly wouldn't go alone, and she certainly wouldn't go with her parents, who had offered to take her. She might be a little girl lost—but she certainly wasn't that uncool.

Chapter Three

Her mother, Little Suzy Homemaker, was in the kitchen preparing her favorite quiche when Sarah walked into the house. Emily Collins, her mother's new best friend, had given her a lecture on the evils of eating red meat, so the family was treated to every kind of quiche conceivable six out of seven days of the week. Sarah never thought there would be a time when she'd actually look forward to having fish for dinner once in a while.

"I'm home," she yelled, slinging her books onto the dining room table, a transplant from their old house that looked distinctly out of place in the new one. It was too large, too dark, and too old-fashioned. Just like Sarah.

Sarah had dark, almost black hair, deep olive skin, and dark chocolate eyes. Unlike Wendy and Joni, quintessential California girls, tall, blond, and lithe, Sarah was big, brown, and awkward. Even her brother fit in better than she did. At least he was thin, and his eyes were blue.

"Have a good day?" her mother called from the kitchen.

"No," Sarah mumbled.

"That's good," her mother chirped happily.

Sarah slumped down into a dining room chair.

"We're eating early tonight," her mother said before she turned on the electric beaters.

Sarah put her hands over her ears. She hated the whir of

the beaters and the ugly sound they made as they clipped the sides of the metal bowl.

"We're eating early tonight," Sarah whispered to herself as she made a face that mirrored her disgust. "We're eating early every night," she added. Then she put her index finger in her mouth and pretended to gag. Actually, at this point, she really did feel like throwing up. This had been the worst day of her life. Not only had she been embarrassed in front of the whole art class third period, she had also been late for chemistry because she was so upset about art she hadn't heard the bell ring after lunch. She tried to sneak into the chem lab as unobtrusively as possible, but Mr. Burns had caught her, even though his back was to the door, and had screamed at her to go to the office for a late pass. She had slunk out of the room, all eyes on her, and had been too embarrassed to go back to class. Not only would she have to face the art class tomorrow, she'd also have to face Mr. Burns.

Sarah groaned. At this rate she would never make it through the year. She got up and headed for the kitchen to appease both her hunger and her emotional starvation with the most fattening food she could find. She couldn't face another quiche made with fake eggs and cream.

"Emily and Herb invited us to a screening tonight," her mother said as Sarah pillaged the refrigerator. Mr. Collins had some kind of perfunctory job—bookkeeper or accountant or something—at Universal Studios and got free passes to screenings of their new movies. Sometimes he invited her parents to join him and Mrs. Collins, and her parents took this as a sign that they were finally making it.

"What?" Sarah asked.

"I said Herb invited us—"

"I mean what's the name of the movie?"

"Oh the name," her mother said, a little embarrassed. "*Touchdown at Durango Pass,* or something like that, I think."

"Sounds great," Sarah said as she shoved a carrot into her mouth.

"Maybe Herb could get an extra ticket."

"Thanks anyway, Mom, but I have too much homework."

"Maybe Wendy would like to go, too. Wouldn't that be fun for you?"

"Fun?" Sarah asked, sarcastically.

The sarcasm went right over her mother's head. Her mother wasn't really a bad person as mothers went, but she sure wasn't all that bright either.

"Why don't you invite Wendy to sleep over this weekend, hon? You could pop popcorn, rent a video—"

"Shoot heroin," Sarah mumbled as her mother gracefully placed the zucchini quiche in the oven.

"Exactly," Donna Alexander said, totally distracted.

"What did I just say, Mom?" Sarah asked exasperated.

"I'm sorry, Sarah," her mother said, "I was just wondering what I should wear tonight. What did you just say?"

"I said that I do not intend to invite Wendy Collins over this weekend or any other weekend."

"Cooper."

"Cooper?"

"Her name's not Collins. It's Cooper. Collins is her mother's name, but her father's name is Cooper, and Herb didn't adopt Wendy when he married her mother because—"

"I don't care why *Herb* didn't adopt Wendy."

"It's not that he didn't want to, but—"

"Mother—"

"Well, I don't want you to think ill of him."

"Think *ill* of him? I don't think about him at all, believe me."

"The Collinses are our best friends, Sarah."

"What about the Bennetts?"

"Well," her mother said. Then she paused for a moment. "They were our best friends, but I don't think you can really call people your best friends if you live in different places. I mean, if you live thousands of miles away and you hardly ever—I mean when could you—except maybe twice a year at most—see each other?"

"Mom, you've known Mrs. Bennett for twenty-five years. You went to high school together. You've only known Emily Collins for five months."

"Well, remember that song you used to sing in day camp—'Make new friends but kee-eep the old,' " her mother began to sing.

"I don't believe this," Sarah said, stalking out of the kitchen.

"Dinner at six-thirty," her mother called to her, after she finished singing the camp song, of course.

Sarah walked past Doug's room on the way to hers. His door was closed, as usual. He was probably sitting on his bed, his earphones plugged into his ears, listening to U2.

She flung herself down on her bed and closed her eyes. "November, December, January, February, March, April, May, June, July, August," she counted on her fingers. Ten more months. Ten more months of hell.

She must have fallen asleep because she didn't hear her father come home. In fact, she didn't hear anything until her mother called them to the table. By the time her mother called a third time, she was in the bathroom washing her face and hands, trying to wake up.

She walked into the dining area and slumped down on the same chair she had fallen into after school. Her books had been removed, and Suzy Homemaker had set quite a table, despite the fact they were having an early dinner so her parents could rush out to join the best of the west for an evening of adventure and romance.

"I have some good news, folks," her father said holding up his wine glass to make a toast.

"Can't wait to hear it," her mother said as she smiled somewhat vacantly at her father.

Probably still thinking about what to wear, Sarah thought. "Me neither," Sarah said, trying to sound interested.

Doug just stared into space as if he hadn't heard a word his father had said. He tended to take after their mother's side of the family. Nice, but not always present.

"Well, we got the figures for our first six months here, and we really have something to celebrate."

Sarah thought her father sometimes sounded like he took his cues from a TV sitcom. She couldn't believe anyone in his right mind would actually say, "We really have something to celebrate."

"So, it looks like we're here to stay," Roger Alexander said. "Cheers."

"Cheers," her mother said, taking a sip of wine.

"Cheers," Doug said, grabbing his beer.

"Cheers," Sarah said, taking a gulp of water, though she didn't feel much like cheering. She'd have felt a lot better if her father had announced that the airline part his company manufactured wasn't selling so well, and they would have to pull up stakes and move back to Ohio.

"Luckily, we don't have to pull up stakes and go back to Ohio," he said. "I'm really getting to like it here."

Well, Sarah was glad he was happy. Her father had started working as a salesman for Mercury Bolts and had worked his way up to vice president of the company. When the company decided to expand and open a small corporate office in California so they could be closer to the airline industry, the number-one industry in the Los Angeles area, they chose her father to head up the West Coast branch.

So they were all displaced because of one bolt. One little part you could hold in your hand. A part that machines stamped out by the hundreds every day.

"We've all made some very nice friends," her mother

said. "It took a little while, but luckily it's all worked out for the best."

"Don't drink any more wine, Mom, please," Sarah said. She hated it when her mother drank wine, even though she never drank more than one or two glasses at most. But one was enough to start her talking, and two turned her into sentimental mush.

"Oh, Sarah, don't be so . . . so square," her mother giggled.

"She's just having a good time," her father said.

"Could you please pass the salad?" Doug said, reaching in front of Sarah and helping himself.

"Don't be rude, Dougie," Donna Alexander said, giving him a light tap on the hand. "Sarah was just about to pass you the salad, weren't you, dear?"

"No," Sarah mumbled.

"See. All you need is a little patience."

"You know, Donna, I think I've been putting on a little weight lately," her father said, patting his belly, which was, indeed, protruding above his belt.

"Well," she said, eyeing his paunch. "I was going to save this for a birthday surprise, but I can't wait. You are going to love this present. This is *the* best present I've ever gotten for you."

Her mother just sat there and smiled, savoring the suspense.

"Sure you don't want to hold it until Friday?" her father asked, wishing she could just give him his birthday present on his birthday for a change and not on the day she bought it.

"So, guess what it is," her mother commanded.

"A bigger belt," her father said, good-naturedly.

"No, but that's not a bad idea," her mother said frowning. "Maybe you'd rather have a belt," she half whispered, her voice trailing off.

"Of course I wouldn't rather have a belt."

"How do you know? You don't know what I got you."

"Well, what did you get me?"

"Oh, see. He can never wait till his birthday. Always wants to know what I bought him as soon as I give him one little hint that it's something special," her mother said, pleased with herself for having manipulated the situation, though she wasn't really quite sure exactly how she'd done it.

"Tell us what it is, Mom," Sarah said.

"You really want to know?"

"No."

"I took out a family membership at the Longacre Health Spa."

"That's a fantastic idea, Donna," her father said.

"I knew you'd love it," her mother said excitedly. "It's the same one the Collinses belong to."

"Does it have a steam room?" Doug asked.

"I hate health clubs," Sarah said.

"So, Sunday, we can go there together, as a family," her mother said.

Doug looked at all of them for a moment, then he laughed out loud.

Chapter Four

Mr. Hill was as good as his word. The painting class was more or less settled into the bright yellow minibus and on its way to the Temporary Contemporary.

Before they got to the museum, Mr. Hill told them it had been an old warehouse owned by the city and that Frank Gehry, an adventurous California architect, had done such a terrific job of converting it into temporary museum space that everyone had fallen in love with it. Even after the permanent Museum of Contemporary Art was completed last year, the board of the museum decided to keep part of their collection at the Temporary.

It was also the space in which four artists would have extended exhibits during the year. And that, in fact, was one of the reasons they were going. The paintings of an artist named Francesco Clemente were on exhibit now, and Mr. Hill thought he was one of the most important painters of the eighties. He also said that a docent would tell them more about both the artist and his work when they got to the museum.

Of course, when he said "docent," the guys totally broke up. "Doe sent!" Bobby screamed. "What's that supposed to be? A deer, or something? How can an animal explain anything to us?"

"It's not an animal, stupid," Jimmy said. "It's dough

sent. Somebody's gonna give us bread for checking out the exhibit.''

''The kind you eat, or the kind you use to buy something to eat?'' Nick yelled.

Luckily, Mr. Hill had a sense of humor. Sarah could have told them what a docent was, because her aunt had been one at the museum in Youngstown. It was very tiny and, of course, couldn't compare to the one in Cleveland, but nevertheless, her aunt and several of her friends, mostly big contributors to the museum, volunteered to take groups of people around and explain the exhibits to them.

Sarah had gone along three or four times, and she'd learned a lot about various painters. But she'd been convinced her aunt and her aunt's friends were making things up as they went along when one of them explained the significance of a large canvas that was totally black.

While she was thinking about the black canvas and laughing to herself, the bus swerved as it turned a corner, and everyone fell to the left.

''Sorry,'' David said, smiling at her.

He had sat down next to her when they boarded the bus, even though there was an empty seat across the aisle. It was better than having to sit next to Bobby or Jimmy or any of the other cavemen in her class, but she didn't want him to think she really cared whether he sat next to her or not, so she didn't say anything to acknowledge his presence. She just sat as close to the window as possible and stared out of it.

''That's okay,'' she mumbled, pulling away from him even further. She thought it might be her imagination, but he seemed to be sitting a little closer to her than necessary. She didn't want him to think just because he had come to her defense last week he had any right to paw her.

She realized, however, that she had probably hurt his feelings by yanking her shoulder to the left with such disdain, because he slid over to the right as far as he could and just stared straight ahead.

She glanced at him out of the corner of her eye. His hair was tied back into a little ponytail. That did it. He was a geek. A ponytail! He was obviously playing artist. What a phony. He didn't have a bad profile, though. Straight nose, cleft in his chin, high cheekbones. She'd never noticed what color his eyes were because she'd never looked directly at him. His hair was dark like hers, however, so she figured his eyes were probably dark, too. She almost felt like talking to him so she could see for sure, but she decided it wasn't worth it. She didn't want to start anything. She didn't want to hang around with anyone as nerdy as she was. The only thing worse than a dork walking around by herself was two dorks walking around pretending they were glad to be together.

The minibus pulled into a lot across the street from the museum, and the twelve of them leaped out and stretched. Then Mr. Hill led them through the door where they were met by a hip-looking young woman dressed in a long skirt, boots, an oversized sweater, and a duster that matched her skirt and was the same length. Must have put her back a few bucks, Sarah thought as she looked her over. She surely didn't resemble her aunt or any of her aunt's friends. This woman was really put together, from her perfect makeup to her expensive boots.

They assembled in a little area to the right of the exhibits, sat down in folding chairs, and listened, mesmerized, as Michel—pronounced My Kel—told them about the exhibit. Even Muladore and Moderelli were quiet. In fact, when Sarah looked over at them, she saw they were both sitting there with their mouths open, taking in everything Michel was saying.

When Michel finished, she asked for questions. "When I was here a few weeks ago," David said, "I noticed some miniatures that looked like Indian art, and I was wondering if Clemente had spent time in India.''

All the other guys turned to look at him. He might as well have taken down his pants and urinated in front of everybody. Even if any of them had ever been to a museum on his own—which, of course, was unlikely—he never, never would have admitted it.

Sarah was too embarrassed to even listen to Michel's answer, but she could tell by the look on her face that she was impressed by the question even if the rest of them weren't.

"Okay, I'm going to turn you loose now," Michel said, smiling at all of them. "Thanks for listening. If you have any questions as you take in the exhibit, look around for me. I'll be in the gift shop."

"Everyone go at your own pace and meet back at the entrance at noon," Mr. Hill said.

Bobby and Jimmy headed straight for the john, where Sarah knew they would sit in a stall and smoke a cigarette. At least that's what they did when they left art class. She could tell because they came back into class reeking of cigarettes—not always the kind you can buy in stores, either.

Sarah thought she'd stick close to Mr. Hill and maybe get some insights into exactly what this artist was trying to do, because the work they saw in the slides Michel showed them looked pretty weird to her. But Mr. Hill started coughing, broke out into a sweat, and waved her on.

"Don't forget to check out Eric Fischl's work while you're here," he called to her as she walked toward the main exhibit.

Sarah stood by herself in the first room and just stared at the enormous paintings on the walls in front of her. Her art history class had only gone as far as Cezanne. She knew nothing about contemporary art, and she wasn't sure she really liked it very much. Looking at Clemente's work, she wasn't sure she liked it at all. Either the man was a mental defective or he was the sanest human being around because he had gotten all of his aggressions out on his canvases. The sexuality and the violence were so blatant they bothered her. But she was fascinated, too. There was something very strong and very provocative about the work.

She walked into the next room, but three of the kids from her class were in there, so she slipped into the room beyond that where a young couple and their little girl were studying a large triptych that covered one whole wall.

The triptychs she was familiar with were religious paintings from the Middle Ages. There was certainly nothing religious about this work. In fact, on closer inspection, Sarah was shocked. The painting consisted of nude male figures in various poses.

"Look. Look," the little girl, who was about two, shouted, as she ran up to the first panel of the triptych and pointed her index finger at a very large penis.

Sarah froze with embarrassment. So did the little girl's parents.

Finally, the father ran up to her and pointed out a row of little rabbits that created a border at the top of the work. "Look at the bunnies," he said enthusiastically. "Aren't they cute?"

"I don't want to look at the bunnies," the little girl said. "I want to look at the pee pee. I like looking at pee pees."

The father glanced over at Sarah and smiled nervously. The little girl's mother had already disappeared.

Suddenly, someone started laughing. "She's just saying what most people think," David said, still laughing as he stood in the doorway and waved at the little girl.

"You wanna see the pee pee, too?" the little girl asked.

"Sure," David said, advancing into the room.

The father smiled at him in utter relief. "Kids," he said. "You never know what they're gonna say."

"That's what I like about 'em," David said.

The father picked up his little girl and carried her into another room, grateful that he could make a graceful exit.

"Do you like this stuff?" Sarah asked. After all, she had to say something. He was standing there right beside her. She couldn't just totally ignore him. Especially as there was no one else in the room.

"Yeah. I do. I like it a lot," he said. "What's really interesting to me is the way Clemente's been influenced by other artists."

"In what way?"

"Well, this piece, for example," David explained. "In this piece you can see Matisse's influence in the form, the motion—"

He stopped.

"Go on," she said.

"Do you really want to hear this?"

"Yeah."

David pointed to various parts of the painting and it began to take on a totally different meaning for her. She began to look at it more objectively, to see it through his eyes. Gradually, she was less repelled by what she saw and more intrigued with it.

When he led her into another room that housed the miniatures he had asked Michel about earlier, Sarah became a convert. The paintings were intricate and exquisite. Every brush stroke was painstakingly singular and distinct, every tiny eye or hand perfectly reproduced, unlike the nudes he had brushed in with such broad strokes when he had painted the grotesques in the other rooms.

"These are marvelous," she said, leaning over to inspect one of the paintings more closely.

"I think it's interesting that he's really saying the same things here, only he used a different form," David said.

Sarah turned to look at him, confused. These paintings were nothing like the other ones. She looked back at the one in front of her. She blushed. When she really looked closely, it did share the same erotic theme as the triptych. David pointed out the similarities to her in a totally scientific, analytical way. He wasn't the least bit embarrassed, either about his knowledge of the art or about the blatant homosexuality of the paintings. And after Sarah pulled herself together and shook off her own embarrassment, she realized she was not only impressed by what he was saying, she agreed with him.

"So you wanna go look at the Fischl paintings?" he asked as they exited the Clemente exhibit.

"Sure," she said. "Maybe you can tell me why Mr. Hill said my stuff was like his."

"Maybe," David said, smiling at her.

They found an Eric Fischl painting, and Sarah almost leaped out of her skin with excitement. She hadn't painted anything as large as the canvas in front of her, but she used the same kinds of muted colors and the same re-creations of realistic forms, she thought as she stared at the nude figures lounging on the boat in the middle of the ocean. Suddenly, she realized why she had instinctively placed the figures in her own paintings in odd, off-center positions. Probably for the same reason Fischl did—to show that this idealistic scene was off kilter. If you studied the painting carefully, you realized the people in the calm, relaxing scene were headed toward a disaster for which they were totally unprepared.

"He's incredible," Sarah said, moved by the complexity of the work. "I only wish I could paint like that."

David smiled at her and pointed to another Fischl painting nearby.

She smiled back at him. His eyes weren't brown like hers. They were gray. Not bluish gray like most gray eyes. A firm, dark gray, almost like slate. And he had long black lashes that curled up at the ends. Funny she had never noticed that before. He was also taller than she was. About two inches taller, which was a tremendous relief. She knew it wasn't supposed to be any big deal if a guy was shorter than a girl. After all, look at Michael Tucker and Jill Eikenberry on "L.A. Law." And they were married in real life, too. Only when she stood next to guys who were shorter than she was, it made her feel even more awkward than she usually felt. She'd try to lean into her spine and make herself shorter, which only made her feel more like a big klutz than ever.

When they climbed back into the bus, David sat down beside her again. Only this time she didn't stare out the window. They were so busy talking about the exhibit she didn't even notice when the bus rolled onto the freeway. It was only when it swerved to the right and she fell against David's shoulder that she remembered where they were and that they were on their way back to school.

Of course, nothing escaped Bobby Muladore,

"Those pictures turn you guys on, or something?" he asked when they climbed out of the bus and walked toward school.

"Or something," David said laughing, but she could tell he was embarrassed. She was mortified.

She hurried away from them and headed for her locker. She had five minutes before afternoon classes began, and she hadn't eaten lunch yet. Most of the guys had brought their lunches with them and had eaten on the bus on the way back from the museum, but she had been too nervous to eat in front of David, so she had said she wasn't hungry when he had offered her part of his sandwich.

Now she was starving, and she was angry with herself for being so stupid. Why was she embarrassed to eat in front of David? He was just some nobody like she was. And why should she care what Bobby Muladore or anyone else thought about her? They were a bunch of primates. They were totally stupid and insensitive. They were so full of it. But they were also the most popular guys at Longacre High. It didn't take too many brains to figure that one out.

"Sarah," David called to her as she closed her locker.

She pretended she hadn't heard him, and she walked down the hall in the opposite direction.

He didn't call her name again, and he didn't run to catch up with her. She guessed he'd gotten the message so she wouldn't have to spell it out for him. She couldn't afford to hang around with him. It was hard enough for her here as it was. Now Muladore and Moderelli would probably make her life more miserable than ever when Mr. Hill left the room.

Still, she wished she had more guts. She wished it didn't matter to her what other people thought. She liked David. She actually liked the guy. In fact, she liked him a lot.

Chapter Five

Sarah lumbered into Ms. Colburn's office after school to find out what she had missed in social studies while she was on the field trip to the museum. They were doing a unit on ethics, which was more or less shooting the breeze, seeing who could sling the most bull during a class session, so she figured she probably hadn't missed much.

As soon as she walked through the door, she was sorry she had come, but before she could go back out again, Ms. Colburn called to her. "Come on in, Sarah. I was just giving David some handouts from this morning. He's in my second period class. This is David Light. David, meet Sarah Alexander. She's in my first period class," Ms. Colburn said, introducing them.

Neither of them mentioned that they already knew each other. They both just smiled awkwardly and turned back toward Ms. Colburn as quickly as possible.

"Okay, so I was telling David that we began a section on AIDS today, which happens to be a subject he's very interested in—"

"I bet," Sarah mumbled sarcastically.

"Excuse me," Ms. Colburn said.

"I said, 'I bet,' " Sarah said more clearly. "Lots of people are interested in it. I mean, you can't pick up a newspaper without seeing at least one article on the subject."

"That's true," Ms. Colburn said, "but it hasn't really seemed to penetrate as far as kids are concerned. I was kind of surprised to learn that most of my students think it really won't affect their lives in any way at all. In fact, they were rather disappointed that we were going to take the time to talk about it."

Sarah wasn't particularly interested in the subject either, for that matter. The only reason she knew there were articles about it was because she'd heard her father moan at least a dozen times, "What more is there to say about this subject? Don't the papers have anything else to write about? I'm really getting tired of reading about AIDS all the time."

She'd never in a million years say that to Ms. Colburn, however. Instead she said, "I think it's kind of interesting. I guess it's something we should learn about."

"Well, I guess so, too," Ms. Colburn said, smiling at her. "Here are a few articles I copied. Read them over tonight. We're going to talk about them tomorrow."

"Thanks," Sarah said, reaching for the articles.

"Wait a minute. I just had an idea. I'd like you to lead the class discussion in first period and David to lead the discussion in second period tomorrow."

"Oh no," Sarah said quickly.

"Why not?"

"I don't really know enough to do that."

"You'll learn," Ms. Colburn said, pointing to the articles that Sarah held clenched in her fist.

"I'd be too embarrassed."

"Oh come on. It'll be a good experience."

"It would be a terrible experience."

"David'll help you out. We do this all the time in honors class. He led a discussion the week before last on abortion."

"Ms. Colburn—do I have to?" Sarah moaned.

"Yeah," Ms. Colburn said, smiling at Sarah. "You do. Now get out of here, you two. I have a ton of papers to grade."

As Sarah walked out of Ms. Colburn's office, she realized David hadn't said one word. She could hear his footsteps behind her, and she almost wanted to turn around,
smile at him, and thank him for—well—being so terrific
this morning at the museum and on the bus ride back to
school. Damn. She wished she could explain it to him. She
wished she could tell him it wouldn't do any good to be seen
with her, either. He led the discussion last week on abortion! She shook her head. What a geek. He probably volunteered to do it. Even in honors classes it wasn't cool to be
that interested in school.

"You taking the twelve?" David asked when she stopped
in front of the bus stop.

"Yeah," she answered, nervously.

"Me, too."

"Ah huh."

"You live north of the freeway, then, I guess."

"Six blocks."

"I'm going to St. Francis."

"Are you sick?"

"To visit my dad."

"Oh."

"Here it comes."

"Yeah."

They boarded the bus together. David sat down next to
her but was careful to keep his distance.

"So—" they both said at the same time.

"You first," he said.

"That's okay. What were you going to say?"

"Nothing. Just that it's not so bad leading a class discussion. All you have to do is sort of introduce the material
and ask a question, then everyone else sort of starts talking,
and before you know it, the period's over."

"We didn't do things like that in my old school."

"Longacre's supposed to be progressive, I guess. That's

why we're doing this ethics unit. I don't know. I think it's interesting—all the stuff we talk about.''

"You think lots of things are interesting. Art. AIDS. Abortion. You're obviously smart. You're in at least one honors class.''

"Accident. It was the only time I could take social studies.''

"Somehow I don't quite buy that. What about English?''

"Well, it's only 'cause my teacher last year pushed me into it. And am I ever sorry. There's way too much reading in that class.

"Yeah, but I bet you're real interested. Right?''

"Wrong. We're reading *Heart of Darkness*. I keep telling myself it's a great book, but I can't keep my eyes open when I try to read it. It took me two hours to get through five pages last night.''

"What else are you taking?''

"Just physics, calc, and fourth year German.''

"Oh—*just* physics, calc, and German?''

"That's all.''

"You forgot art.''

"That's for fun. I'm not good at it, or anything. I just play around with the paints.''

"Your schedule's as full as mine is.''

"Unfortunately. I wanted to drop German so I'd have some free time, but then I figured, what the hell, I've taken it three years, it's stupid to drop it now.'' He paused for a moment. "Well, that's not exactly why I didn't drop it. Klinger said it would look good on my college transcript.''

"Oh, God—don't even talk about that. Every time I think about filling out those stupid applications I have an anxiety attack.''

"I know what you mean.''

"If I don't get into Ohio State, I'll die.''

"Why Ohio State?''

"I used to live there. All my friends are going."

"Oh," he said, disappointed.

Sarah was disgusted. Just when they were having this perfectly nice conversation, he showed his true colors. She was sure he was disappointed because she wasn't applying to a prestigious school like Berkeley. Most of the top students at Longacre were trying to get into either Berkeley or UCLA, according to Mrs. Collins. Except those who were smart enough or rich enough or both to apply to Ivy League schools. Wendy was going to Arizona State—if she could get in.

"Why the 'Oh'?"

"Sorry. Just thinking out loud. I—I guess I thought you'd be going to an art school."

"Why?" she asked, shocked.

"Because you have talent. You're really, really good. Even Mr. Hill thinks so."

"I'm not that good," she said, but she couldn't help being pleased by the compliment.

"I think you are."

"Thanks," she said softly.

"But—maybe Ohio State has a good art department," he said.

"I don't know. Maybe. Where do you want to go to school?"

"I applied to Brown—early action."

"Brown? Early action?"

"Brown," he said, laughing. "It's in Rhode Island."

"Never heard of it."

"It's pretty good."

"How come you applied there?"

"That's where my dad went to school."

"What's early action?"

"If you know what your first-choice school is, and you think you have a chance of getting in, you can apply early, and they let you know early before your applications have to be in for most other schools.''

''Guess that saves you a lot of trouble. Think you'll get in?''

''Hope so,'' he said, getting up. ''This is my stop.''

''See you.''

He turned to look at her as if he was about to say something. Then he changed his mind and walked to the front of the bus.

He smiled at her when she looked out the window at him. Then he crossed the street. She turned in her seat and watched him walk up the driveway of St. Francis.

He was so easy to talk to. She almost felt comfortable with him. And he was cute. Very cute. Nice build, too. If only he weren't so interested in everything. If only he were just normal like all the other kids.

Chapter Six

"You left your books on the dining room table again," Suzy Homemaker shouted to Doug as he got into his car.

"I'm late. Just shove them on the floor. I'll pick them up when I get back," he said revving up his motor.

"Shove them on the floor," Donna Alexander said to herself as Sarah walked past her and into the house.

Sarah put her own books on the table next to Doug's, then headed into the kitchen to grab something to eat before she went to her room to look at the articles for social studies.

"I am so tired of picking up after everybody," her mother announced. "When you come into the house, put your books in your room. I don't know what's wrong with you kids. It's only a few more feet to your rooms."

"I'm going. I'm going," Sarah said, grabbing a bran muffin, another of Mrs. Collins's musts. They used to have cookies and brownies at their house in the old days. Now it was granola bars and bran muffins.

Her mother began picking up Doug's books as Sarah poured herself a glass of juice. As she walked into the dining area to pick up her own books, her mother was looking at a paper that had fallen out of Doug's notebook.

"Something from his computer programming class," her

mother said absentmindedly as she turned the paper over to check the grade on the other side.

"Mom! Put the paper back. You shouldn't be checking up on him."

"I can't find the grade."

"Just put it away. He'll really be pissed if he finds out you were looking at it."

"Then he shouldn't have left it on the table," her mother said slowly as she continued to study the paper in front of her.

"He didn't leave it on the table. He left it in his book."

"Sarah, has Douglas said anything to you about having a girlfriend?"

"No," Sarah said wrinkling her brow. Doug had been going out a lot lately and was much more pleasant around the house, but she didn't know anything about a girlfriend.

"Well, it looks like he has one."

"What do you mean?"

"There's a note from her on this paper."

"Let's see," Sarah said, trying to look over her mother's shoulder.

Her mother put her hand over the top of the paper. "Thought you said we shouldn't be checking up on him," she said chuckling.

"This is different."

"It's worse."

"Mom!"

"I think you're right. We shouldn't be snooping."

"But you already snooped, and besides he's so closed-mouthed we'll never learn who she is from him. He never tells anybody anything."

Her mother took her hand away from the top of the paper and giggled just like a little kid. "Don't say a word about this," she warned. "He'll tell us when he's ready."

"Loved last night," the note read. "Can't wait to see you again." It was signed, "Terry."

"Wow," Sarah said laughing. "I didn't think the guy had it in him."

"Your brother's a very handsome young man."

"I agree. Only he's more interested in computers than he is in women."

"Well, it looks like this one combines both his interests. She must be in his computer class."

"Good for him," Sarah said.

"Probably why he ran off so fast," her mother said. "Phone rang. He answered it, and he was out of here two minutes later."

"God, I wish I could ask him about her. I'm so curious. Aren't you?"

"Douglas is a big boy now. He has the right to some privacy," her mother said with a straight face. Then she totally broke up laughing. "Emily Collins is going to go crazy. She told me Wendy has a crush on Doug."

"Oh my God. I hope he has better taste than that."

"Wendy is a darling girl."

"Wendy's a pig."

"I really wish you wouldn't talk that way."

"It's the truth."

"Sarah, if you can't—"

"Say anything nice, then don't say anything at all," Sarah said, finishing the sentence for her mother.

"That's not very amusing."

"Not meant to be," Sarah said, grabbing her books and walking off.

Suddenly, she was in a very bad mood. Now everyone in her family had a best friend here except her. She didn't mind going to a movie on Friday night with Doug. Since none of the kids at school, except Wendy and Joni, knew him, the kids would think he was her date if they saw them together. Now who was she going to go out with?

She sat down on her bed and took out the articles Ms. Colburn had given her. AIDS might be a matter of life and death to some people, but right now finding out how to survive for ten more months in Longacre was *her* uppermost priority.

As she began reading, however, she realized that other people's problems were even worse than hers. The statistics were rather shocking. She had been wrong about AIDS. It wasn't just a disease that homosexuals and intravenous drug users got. Anyone could get it. She could get it if she had sex with someone who had the AIDS virus. Of course, she wasn't planning on that. She wasn't planning on having sex with anyone until *the* right person came along. Especially after reading this stuff.

She heard the front door slam and Doug call out to her mother, "I just came home to grab some cash, Mom. I won't be here for dinner."

"Where are you going Dougie?" her mother asked innocently.

"Out, Mom."

"To meet a friend?"

"No."

"You're going to have dinner out by yourself? What's the matter? Don't you like what we're having? You don't even know what we're having."

Sarah heard Doug laugh.

"My friend's waiting for me in the car."

"Well, my goodness, why didn't you say so? You know there's always room for another person at our table. Invite her to come in. I mean, what kind of manners do you have leaving your friend sitting in the car while you come into the house?"

"See you, Mom," Doug said.

"Aren't you staying for dinner?"

"Nope."

Sarah heard a car horn. This girlfriend of his is sure impatient, she thought.

"Be out in a sec, Terry," Doug called.

Sarah smiled to herself. Well, at least they knew her name.

"Have fun," she heard her mother say. She had obviously walked to the door so she could get a look at Terry. Sarah knew her mother wouldn't be able to resist that.

As soon as she heard the car pull out, she tossed her books aside and ran into the living room. Her mother was still standing at the front window, staring out into the street.

"We were wrong," her mother said softly.

"What do you mean?"

"About Doug."

"No, we weren't. I heard him say this Terry person was in the car. Didn't I?"

"Yeah."

"Well?"

"Terry's just a friend. Not a girlfriend."

"Yeah. Well, it sure didn't sound like it from that note."

"We just jumped to conclusions."

"How could you tell she was just a friend by looking at her? Is she ugly, or something?"

"Terry's not a she. Terry's a he."

Sarah looked at her mother for a moment, then started laughing uncontrollably. It started as a little giggle, then it erupted into a spasm, and finally it overtook her and she fell on the floor laughing so hard she could barely breathe.

"Oh, God. He really put one over on us. He probably left the damn paper there on purpose. He knew we'd read the note. What a riot. I love it. You got to give it to the guy. He has a real sense of humor," she gasped, still laughing.

"I guess Wendy is still in the running then," her mother said.

"I don't think so, Mom. Wendy Collins. Wendy Collins," Sarah gasped. Then she began to oink. She sat on the floor laughing and oinking until tears rolled out of her eyes.

"I'm glad you think it's so funny," her mother said, walking out of the room and leaving her there by herself. "And I told you, her name's not Collins," she yelled from the kitchen.

"Wendy Collins," Sarah said again. "What a porker."

Chapter Seven

"So how was school today?" her father asked when they sat down to dinner. It was the same question he had asked her every day since she had started kindergarten. When she was in elementary school she would recap the day's events for him with great enthusiasm, trying not to forget the smallest details. Now she more or less shrugged off his question knowing he really wasn't listening to her answer, anyway. While she was talking, it just gave him time to drift off and think about his accounts or about a problem at the office while he stared at her, pretending to take in every word she said. He was an expert at it. It had taken her years to realize he really wasn't listening even though he was sitting right in front of her, looking straight into her eyes.

"We went to the Temporary Contemporary," she said.

"That's nice."

She smiled to herself. How would he know if that was nice, or not? He'd never been there. He probably didn't even know what it was.

He smiled at her. "And how's the work going?"

"Fine."

"That's good."

"You see, I told you school wouldn't be any more difficult for you here than it was in Ohio," her mother said.

"It's easier," Sarah admitted. School work was not the problem in her life. She was, in fact, surprised that her old school had prepared her so well. She wasn't in honors classes, but she did very well in the classes she was in. She had learned to write—correctly and carefully—and was amazed at the difficulty most of the other students had with their essays. Not that they wrote that many. In fact, since the beginning of school, they had written only two. In Ohio they wrote one a week.

"You know what I'm going to do tonight?" her father asked. "I am going to finally get to those photos."

"Sure you are," Sarah said.

"That's good, dear," her mother said. Her mother was a total literalist. At least once a week, since last May, her father had been saying he was going to get to the photo albums and update them. Before they moved, they had carted out boxes of family pictures from the last fifteen years. "This is terrible," her father had said. "Someone should have put these pictures into albums years ago. This is our whole family history. These pictures are very valuable."

They had all agreed and said that because the pictures were so valuable and because he was so well organized, he was elected to do the job.

Obviously, with all the moving arrangements, it hadn't gotten done before they left Ohio. And with the settling in arrangements at home and in her father's new office, it hadn't gotten done since they'd moved to California, either.

To her surprise, however, as soon as dinner was over and the table was cleared, her father brought out the boxes of pictures and several albums he had purchased that afternoon and went to work while Sarah and her mother were doing the dishes.

"Want to help, pumpkin?" he asked when she walked out of the kitchen.

"Have too much work to do," she answered. But she stopped to take a look at the pictures he was slipping into the plastic pockets of the book.

"Is that me or Doug?"

"Doug. It's amazing how much you two looked alike when you were babies, though, isn't it?"

"We *are* siblings."

"I kept telling your mother to cut off those curls so people wouldn't think he was a girl."

"Look—it's the park on Todd Lane. Remember you guys used to take us there all the time to see the swans?"

"One in a stroller and one in a back carrier," her father said sighing. "Those were the days."

"Yeah."

"Remember the time you and Doug were feeding the swans and one of them came right up to you and ate out of your hand?"

"Yeah," Sarah said laughing.

"You were afraid he might bite you, but you were too fascinated to pull your hand away."

"Here's a picture of it—of me holding my hand out to the swan. And here's another one of me with the swan eating out of my hand," she said rummaging through the pictures on the table. "Ohhhh, I was so cute then."

"You still are."

"Sure," she said sarcastically.

"I think you are."

"You're my father. You don't count."

"Thanks a lot."

"Every father thinks his daughter's cute."

"Well, to tell you the truth," he said, squinting as he looked at her, "I don't really think you're cute."

"What!"

"Cute is for little kids with freckles. I do think you're turning into a beautiful young woman, though."

"Turning into one, huh? With this mop of hair I can't

even comb out? With this nose that is bigger than Doug's? He should have been the female child in the family. He's the one who's beautiful, not me.''

"You're too hard on yourself, Sar. You're big boned, but your eyes are fabulous. You've got a great figure—''

"I'm eight pounds overweight.''

"That's a recent addition,'' he said nodding in her mother's direction. "What do you say, Mother? Think you could substitute yogurt for sour cream when you make those quiches?''

"I never thought of that,'' her mother said, walking into the dining area to join them.

"Okay, that'll take care of the weight. And maybe your mother can get the name of a good hairdresser from Emily. That'll take care of the hair. Actually, I know some people who would kill for hair like yours,'' he said rubbing the bald spot on the top of his head.

"Anyone in particular?'' she asked laughing.

He was okay. She knew he cared about her even if he wasn't always available.

"Nobody I know,'' he said. "Hey, I thought you had too much homework to help me.''

"I do. Honest. It's just hard to tear myself from these pictures. It's so much fun looking at them.''

"They'll still be here tomorrow,'' her father said.

"Yeah, but will I still be here tomorrow?'' she joked, as she walked back to her room. "Ohio's still looking pretty good to me,'' she said, closing her door and smiling to herself.

She loved looking through the old pictures. They brought up all kinds of memories. Good memories. Memories about times when she was happy. When they were a real family and did things together. Now everyone seemed to be going in separate directions.

She picked up the AIDS material again and started taking notes on a recent article in the *Los Angeles Times* about a biology course at UCLA. The course was going to deal with the issue of AIDS for a whole quarter. It looked like the students at UCLA were a lot more interested in the subject than the kids at Longacre were. More than two thousand of them had tried to enroll. Finally five hundred and fifty were admitted. The article went on to say that the professor teaching the course had decided he wanted to introduce it into the curriculum because three of his colleagues and eighteen students he knew had died from AIDS. That was pretty shocking. Sarah didn't know anybody who had ever died from AIDS, or anyone who even had it, for that matter. Her parents didn't know anyone who had it, either. They'd heard rumors about someone they vaguely knew in Youngstown, but nothing was ever verified, and when the guy had died, she remembered her father's reading his obituary and saying that the man, whose name she had long forgotten, had died of pneumonia.

Sarah shivered. Maybe it really was a plague, she thought as she read on.

She was both fascinated and frightened by the material she read. Though she still felt insecure about standing up in front of her class tomorrow, and she still considered trying to talk Ms. Colburn out of making her do it, she knew she was prepared to, at least, get the discussion going, and if no one talked, she had enough information to keep it going for a while.

She heard her mother walk into her bedroom and close the door. Her father would be locking up the front of the house and turning off the lights—except for the hall light and the one in front of the house, which he would leave on for her brother who hadn't come home yet. She looked at her clock. It was almost eleven. Some dinner. He and his friend must have gone to a party afterward.

A minute later she heard her brother's car pull into the driveway, but she didn't hear his car door slam. She sat poised listening for it. Nothing. That was strange, she thought. He always pulled into the driveway and slammed out of the car a few minutes later, then unlocked the front door, walked into the kitchen, grabbed something from the refrigerator, and walked back to his room with it.

Suddenly, she heard her father let out a stream of invectives and she jumped off of her bed in shock. Her father never swore. He hated to hear her and her brother swear. He even hated it when they said hell or damn, but he had just let loose with words that even the most adventurous kids at her school shied away from.

Something's happened to Doug, she thought. Something terrible. He was in an accident. That wasn't his car that had pulled into the driveway. It must have been a police car. They've come to tell us Doug's in the hospital. That he's in a coma. That he's dead.

By this time she was in the living room, which was dark except for the light shining in through the window. Her father was standing in front of the window shaking. She ran up to him.

"Dad—Daddy—what!"

"Go back to your room. Now!" her father commanded. She had never heard him talk like that. He had never yelled at her before.

"I—" she started to say as her mother ran into the living room, pulling her bathrobe around her.

"What is it, Roger?" she asked, obviously just as panicked as Sarah.

"Both of you get out of here. Now. Right now!" he shouted at them as they backed off and retreated down the hallway to their bedrooms.

"I'll handle this," they heard him say as Sarah and her mother huddled together in the doorway of her parents' bedroom.

They stood there shaking. For the first time that she could remember, her father didn't sound as if he could handle anything.

Chapter Eight

They could hear the tension in her father's voice, but they couldn't understand what he was saying because he was whispering. It seemed as if they had stood huddled together forever, but she knew they had only been there for a few minutes. Finally, her father raised his voice, and she heard him say, "Not in my house, you won't. I want you out of here now. Right now! You can get your things tomorrow. They'll be outside the front door."

Sarah couldn't imagine what horrible crime her brother had committed. What could he have done to make their father angry enough to throw him out of the house like that? Doug didn't even have a job—a place to go. What would he do? She flashed on an image of the homeless people who slept in doorways in downtown L.A. or in tents at the beach. Would that happen to her brother? And why? Why?

She turned to her mother. Her mother must have heard it, too. Donna Alexander was in shock. She stood staring into space for a moment, then she broke loose from Sarah and rushed back into the living room. Sarah followed after her.

Just as they got to the dining area, she heard a car peel out of the driveway and race to the corner.

"What?" her mother asked her father as he stood in the middle of the room unable to move.

He didn't answer her.

"What, Roger? What happened?"

"I don't know. I don't know," he said anguished.

"What did he do?"

"I don't want to talk about it," her father said, sinking down onto the couch in front of the fireplace like a man who had just been handed a death sentence.

"But where is he? Where did he go?" her mother begged.

"I don't know," her father said, his head in his hands.

"Roger! What did he do to you?"

"Nothing. He didn't do anything to me. Just go to bed. Both of you. Go to bed while I sort this thing out."

"What thing, Daddy?"

"Go to bed, Sarah," he said sharply, as if he were punishing her. As if it were her fault—whatever it was that had provoked him to send his son flying out of the house and into the night with nowhere to go.

"How can you expect me to go to bed? What am I supposed to do? Just pretend you and Doug had your annual fight, and you'll make up tomorrow like you always do? I heard you. I heard you tell him you'd put his clothes outside the house so he can sneak up and grab them like some animal."

"He is an animal," her father whispered without looking at her.

Sarah shivered. Her father had turned down the heat as usual before coming to bed, and the temperature had dropped. She was wearing a nightgown and no robe, and the cold began to creep up her bare feet to her legs. She put her arms around her body to warm herself up, but it didn't help much. She felt chilled to the bone.

"Go to bed, sweetheart," her mother said softly, her own teeth chattering, though Sarah wasn't sure it was from the cold. She walked over to Sarah, put her arm around her, and whispered, "Go. We'll talk about it in the morning."

She didn't know what else to do, so she turned and walked back to her room. She got under the covers, but she couldn't warm up even though she put one cold foot against her leg until it warmed up, then put it down and slid the other one up.

She strained to hear what her parents were saying, but they were talking too softly. She knew her mother was crying now, but she didn't know if her mother knew any more than she had when they walked into the living room.

She lay awake for a long time. Finally, she heard her mother's footsteps coming toward her room. She heard her go into the bathroom. She heard the water run. But she didn't hear her father's footsteps. She couldn't fall asleep until she heard him walk to the back of the house. She didn't know why exactly. It was just sort of a bargain she had made with herself. When she heard him walk into his room and close the door, she would allow herself to fall asleep.

She wanted to reach over for her headphones and plug herself into a tape that could take her away, but if she did that she wouldn't be able to hear him. So she just lay there forcing herself to think about her social studies assignment.

She began to form the questions she would ask the class during the discussion. She forced herself to concentrate on the articles she had read and not on what she had heard a few minutes ago.

After a while she almost convinced herself that she had dreamed it up. That her father was in bed, and her brother hadn't pulled into the driveway yet.

The tension in her neck began to ease, and she could feel her shoulders relax. Half-asleep, she convinced herself that everything would be all right in the morning. Doug had done something to make her father really angry, but whatever it was, it couldn't have been that bad.

Suddenly, she bolted upright. She was wide awake, but she didn't know why at first. Then she sniffed. She sniffed again. Smoke. The house was on fire.

"Help," she yelled. "Mom. Dad. Smoke," she yelled

as she jumped out of bed and ran down the hallway to her parents' bedroom, forgetting everything she had learned about what to do in an emergency. Her mother was already at the door calling to her father. "Fire. Call the fire department, Roger!"

"It's only me," her father yelled from the living room. "I'm burning something in the fireplace."

Rubbing her eyes, she walked into the living room to see what was going on.

Her father was kneeling down in front of the fireplace, ripping pages out of a book and throwing them into the fire. What was going on here, she wondered. She glanced over at the logs in a neat pile next to the fireplace.

She watched page after page go into the flames, which now danced to a rhythm of their own.

Sarah walked over to the couch, sat down next to it, and leaned over to see what her father was using to build his holocaust. She gasped. He was burning the pages from the photo album he had been working on.

"What are you doing?" she screamed.

She ran over to him and tried to pry the album out of his hands before he could toss any more pictures into the flames. But he held on to the album as he watched the photographs curl, blacken, then disappear into ashes.

"Daddy!"

"Roger! Stop it!"

"You're burning our family pictures," Sarah yelled.

"That was our old family," he said calmly, so calmly that despite the heat rising up from the fireplace, despite the flush on her face from the flames, she was colder than she'd ever been in her entire life.

Chapter Nine

She was so tired she didn't even notice Mr. Hill wasn't sitting on his desk waiting for them to file into the classroom. When she had gotten up this morning, she had decided not to go to school, but she had changed her mind for two reasons. First of all, if she didn't show up for social studies, Ms. Colburn would think that either she was too chicken to get up in front of the class or that she hadn't prepared for the challenge. For some reason she didn't want her to think that. So she had gotten out of bed and trudged into the kitchen hoping a cup of coffee would wake her up.

In the kitchen she ran into the second reason for going to school. Her father was standing at the counter in his bathrobe, smoking a cigarette, something he hadn't done in five years. His smoking was bad enough. His being there was worse. By seven o'clock he was always on the freeway heading for his office. His being in the kitchen must mean he was staying home from work today. She wanted to ask him about last night. She wanted to know just what crime her brother had committed that was so terrible his own father had thrown him out of the house. She wanted to know where Doug was. She wanted to tell her father he had scared her. But she didn't tell him anything, and she didn't ask him anything. She didn't even get one word out because as soon as she opened her mouth, he said there would be no discussion about last night. Then her father had picked up his cup of coffee and walked out of the kitchen.

She hoped that meant what had happened would some-how get resolved while she was at school. And even though she wanted to know what had set her father off, she didn't want to hear the yelling and screaming that was bound to fill the house and half the neighborhood when her brother came home to get his clothes, which she was sure her father would not put in front of the house as he had threatened. She was sure Doug and her father would work things out, but the process they went through before their reconcilia-tions was enough to make her crazy. She remembered the time her parents had come home from a movie and smelled marijuana coming from Doug's bedroom, even though the door was closed and the window was open. She thought her father would never get over that one, but he had. It had taken him a few days, but eventually he had calmed down, and he and Doug had worked it out. So she was sure they would work it out this time, too—even though her father had never actually kicked Doug out of the house before, no matter how angry he had been.

"Where's Hill?" Bobby asked when he bounded into the classroom.

Sarah's head ached. She wished he'd just sit down and shut up.

"I'm subbing for Mr. Hill today," the woman said meekly.

Oh God, this was going to be hell, Sarah thought. It was bad enough to have a sub, but to have one who obviously would not be able to control the class was going to be murder.

Everyone coming through the door asked the same ques-tion, "Where's Hill?"

And everyone got the same answer, followed by a ner-vous smile. It took about three seconds to size her up. As soon as the bell rang and she said she had been told they were supposed to continue working on whatever it was they were working on, they all knew she didn't have a clue about what to do with the class.

"Aren't you gonna take roll, Miss?" Jimmy asked.

"Roll? Oh, yes. Yes, of course," she said, looking into every drawer for the attendance book.

Everyone started to giggle. They all knew there was no attendance book. Even though it was against school policy, Mr. Hill refused to take roll. He figured that students should be in art classes because they wanted to be there, not because they had to be, which was great, theoretically, but didn't always work out practically, especially on days when there was a substitute.

"I can't seem to find the attendance book," she said flushing.

"Maybe he took it home with him," Billy said.

"Yes. Maybe. If one of you could lend me a piece of paper, perhaps we could just pass it around the classroom and you could all sign your names so Mr. Hill will know who was here and who wasn't when he returns."

Silence.

"Excuse me. Does anyone have an extra piece of paper?"

More silence.

Finally, she walked over to Sarah, the only other female in the room, and pleaded with her silently. Sarah looked at the sub without making any effort to help her out even though she felt sorry for her. She couldn't afford to be a do-gooder, however. She had a hard enough time in this class, as it was.

"Could you give me a sheet of paper, please?" the substitute teacher asked, obviously annoyed.

Against her better judgment, Sarah took a sheet of paper out of her notebook and handed it to the teacher.

"Hey, lady, what's your name?" Bobby yelled.

"Bosworth. Mrs. Bosworth," she said as she wrote something on top of the paper. "Now if you'll just put your names under periods three and four, you can all get to work."

Sarah put on her smock and got her canvas out of the closet. She slowly and deliberately squeezed some paints onto her palette, but she didn't touch them. She just stared at them till the colors all blurred together. She wondered if Doug had come back to the house yet. She wondered where he had stayed last night. Maybe he had gone to stay with his friend Terry.

"Look here!" Mrs. Bosworth said, seething. "You may think this is some kind of a joke, but an unexcused absence is no laughing matter. I intend to turn this paper in to the office, and if your names aren't on it, you're going to have one big problem."

Bobby, Billy, and Jimmy snickered.

"You," she said, pointing to Bobby. "What is your name?"

"Mick Jagger."

Billy and Jimmy could barely contain themselves.

"And I suppose you're Elvis?" she said angrily, pointing to Jimmy.

"He's Elvis," Jimmy said, pointing to Bobby. "I'm Prince."

"Fine," Mrs. Bosworth said, sarcastically. "Just fine."

She wasn't sure what to do next so Mrs. Bosworth sat down at Mr. Hill's desk and glared at the class, hoping they'd all either get to work and stop making her life miserable, or just disappear. Mr. Hill never sat at his desk. He worked the room going from student to student, encouraging them to try something new or enhance what they were already working on. He must walk miles during a double period, Sarah thought as she sat staring at Mrs. Bosworth. Suddenly, she missed him. He never said that much, but his presence was comforting, and not just because the guys acted like Cro-Magnons when he left the room, either. He had a certain calmness and patience, a love for what he was doing. And he transmitted that to the class. Even Bobby and Jimmy responded to him, though they both pretended they had no interest at all in what he said. She had noticed though. She had seen them both listen very carefully to his comments.

Mrs. Bosworth must have felt Sarah staring at her. She opened a book and pretended to read. Sarah knew she was only pretending because the book was upside down. Mrs. Bosworth was doing exactly what Sarah did when she wanted to hide from the world.

Sarah turned toward the back of the room to look for David, but no one stood in front of his easel. She suddenly missed him, too. What was going on here? It was as if the whole world was turned upside down. Instead of seeing her brother at breakfast, her father had been there. Instead of feeling Mr. Hill's calm presence in the room, some nervous old lady was sending out all kinds of negative vibrations and putting everyone on edge. She could feel the underlying rumble of mischief building around her. She just prayed that this Mrs. Bosworth wouldn't get totally freaked out and walk out the door leaving her alone with these animals.

"So what's with Hill? He got the flu, or something?" Bobby asked.

"I don't know," Mrs. Bosworth said without looking up from her book.

"Maybe he's got a bad virus, or something," Jimmy said. "He looked sick yesterday. Didn't he, you guys?"

"Yeah," they all said, laughing.

Sarah didn't laugh with them. Even though they were joking around, it was true. Mr. Hill had looked sick yesterday. Sicker than usual.

"I think I caught it," Bobby said, grabbing his stomach and pretending to throw up.

"Me, too," Jimmy said, imitating Bobby.

"Me, too," Billy said, falling to the floor and thrashing around.

"That's enough!" Mrs. Bosworth said, getting up from the desk and walking over to Bobby.

"Better get away from me or you'll get it too, lady."

"I don't know what you think you're doing, but whatever it is, it isn't very funny."

"Who said sick is funny?" Bobby said. "It ain't funny. It's sick," he said trying to keep a straight face. The other guys got hysterical.

"I just want to tell you one thing," Mrs. Bosworth said, shaking with anger. "I understand that Mr. Hill will be out for quite some time. Now I was asked to take his classes temporarily until Miss McAllister could find someone to fill in on a more permanent basis, but—"

"What do you mean he'll be out for quite some time?" Bobby said, forgetting all about his stomachache.

"He's in the hospital."

Everyone started talking at once.

"What's wrong?" Jimmy asked.

"Whoa—what's he in for?" Bobby wanted to know.

"He have an operation, or something?" Billy asked, getting up from the floor.

"I don't know any of the details," Mrs. Bosworth said coldly. This was more like it. She finally had their attention.

"Well, when's he gonna be back? That's what we'd like to know," Bobby said.

"I told you. I don't know any of the details."

"What if they don't find someone else?"

"Then I'll have to stay here until they do—if I have some cooperation. If I decide not to come back, you'll all be placed in study halls," Mrs. Bosworth said with satisfaction.

"Screw that," Bobby said under his breath.

Jimmy and Billy picked up their art supplies and started sorting them out at their desks.

The room got very quiet. "Well, is he *really* sick, or something?" Bobby asked finally. "I mean, he didn't have a heart attack, or anything, did he?"

"I don't know—"

"Yeah, yeah—you don't know any of the details," Bobby said, but the usual defiance was missing from his voice.

Chapter Ten

The drizzle kept everyone inside the cafeteria during lunch period, except for the truly antisocial kids who brought their lunches and ate by themselves in their cars.

Sarah picked up a tray and walked through the line with a tremendous heaviness hanging over her. Not only was she still worried about her brother, but Mr. Hill's absence had thrown her, though she didn't know exactly why. Teachers stayed home from school all the time. Mr. Ronelli, one of her teachers from her old school, used to take a day off every month or so for R and R—racquetball and "restling." He said he had to do that to stay sane. Maybe Mr. Hill was doing that, too. Then again, maybe he wasn't. He wasn't. She knew he wasn't. He was too serious. Not the type for R an R. And besides that, he looked too sick to be staying out for any other reason. And what was this business about his being in the hospital? People didn't go to hospitals unless they were really sick.

She walked past the salads and sandwiches to the hot food. "What'll it be?" one of the hair-netted women behind the counter asked.

Sarah looked at the food, unable to distinguish one dish from another, and pointed to something in the middle tray that looked vaguely like spaghetti and tomato sauce.

The woman dished it up and distractedly pushed the plate to the counter in front of Sarah.

Doesn't anyone give a damn about anything? Sarah wondered as she picked up the plate. She knew working in a school cafeteria wasn't the greatest job in the world, but maybe if the people doing it just stopped to say hi once in a while, it would be a little less miserable.

Sarah walked to an empty table and put down her tray. She poked the food around for a few minutes, then shoved it away. She didn't feel much like eating. She reached for her book bag, brought it up to the table, and searched for her *Heart of Darkness*.

"Can I sit down?"

She looked up. It was David. She felt relieved. No, that wasn't it. She felt more than relieved. She felt happy. Very happy to have someone sitting across the table from her. Happy, in fact, that the someone was David.

"You weren't in art class this morning."

"I know. Ms. Colburn wanted me to lead the discussion in her third and fourth period classes, too. Hill said it was okay with him.

"When'd you talk to him about it?"

"Yesterday."

"He was absent, too."

"Yeah? I thought he looked kind of sick yesterday."

"Me, too."

"Probably the flu."

"He's in the hospital," she said, still concerned about Mr. Hill.

"Must be a bad case," David said, looking a little worried himself. "Still, I'm sure he'll survive," he added to reassure her. "Its going around. Everyone's got it."

"Yeah, I know. All the cave men in the class have it, too," she said laughing.

"They all absent?"

"Only mentally."

"They can be a drag."

"They're so obnoxious."

"They're not so bad. I don't know. I've known Moderelli and Muladore since grade school. They just like to fool around. But it can get on your nerves."

"You guys were friends?"

"Yeah. Used to be. They stopped hanging around with me in high school 'cause I started going to classes while they were sitting in the john getting high."

Sarah laughed. "I knew it. I knew they were going into the john getting high. How come none of the teachers know it?"

"Don't want to, I guess."

"You kidding?"

"No. What are they going to do about it, anyway? Can't police all the bathrooms."

"They should be kicked out of school. They're totally out of control."

"Like I said, they're not bad. Not that bright, but they don't really want to hurt anyone."

"Guess you forgot about what happened in class—"

"I didn't forget. Only I don't think they really wanted to hurt you. They were just teasing. Most of the girls they hang around with don't mind that kind of teasing. I think Moderelli kind of likes you," he added smiling at her.

"He likes me?" she asked, amazed.

"Yeah. He has a crush on you. I see him looking at you all the time."

"Come on."

"I mean it."

"Come on."

"It's true. He's always looking at you when he thinks you won't notice."

"How do you know?"

" 'Cause—"

" 'Cause?"

" 'Cause—" David said turning away from her. "Just " 'cause I know."

"You're making that up so I'll feel better."

" 'Cause I'm always looking at you, too," he said finally.

There was a long embarrassed silence. Sarah could feel her face burn with pleasure.

"Really?" she asked when she could look at him again.

"Yeah. Really. Only you never look at anyone except Mr. Hill."

"I'm too scared to look at anyone else."

"Most people think you're too stuck up."

"Stuck up!"

"Yeah. You never talk to anyone. You walk around with your head in the air or a book under your nose as if you couldn't care less if anyone said hello to you or not, so most people don't bother."

"That's why they don't talk to me?"

"That's part of the reason."

"I thought they didn't like me."

"How could they dislike you? They don't even know you."

"What else don't they like about me?" she asked, still shocked by what she'd just heard.

"You're new."

"That's it?"

"It's hard coming into a new school when you're a senior. Most of us have been together for a long time, and kids just don't like to make room for other kids, I guess. At least most of them don't."

"What about you?"

"Me? I like meeting new people," he said laughing. "But then I'm a bit of a weirdo, in case you haven't noticed."

"I've noticed," she said, feeling better than she'd felt since she'd moved to California.

"I'm not that weird," he said defensively.

"Yes, you are," she joked.

"Then how come you let me sit down at your table?"

"I got tired of sitting by myself."

"Oh," he said, his face dropping.

"I was just kidding."

He smiled at her, and she noticed he had a dimple in his cheek. She liked him. How could she help it? How could anyone help liking him?

"Do the other kids think you're weird?" she asked tentatively.

"Yeah. They do," he said smiling broadly.

"You're proud of it?"

"Of course. Who wants to be like everyone else?"

"I don't know. I don't know," she said laughing. She wondered if she should tell him that was the weirdest thing about him. The fact that he didn't want to be like anyone else. Most kids wanted to be exactly like everyone else. They dressed alike, talked alike, used the same expressions, listened to the same music, liked the same baseball players. Hell, even her parents wanted to be like other people. Why else would they be standing on their heads to please the Collinses?

"So—what do you say?"

"About what?"

"About going to a movie Saturday night?"

"Sure."

"You will?"

"Yeah."

"Okay."

"Okay."

They sat and smiled at each other for a moment, then both of them started to giggle self-consciously.

"How'd it go in social studies this morning?" he asked finally.

"How'd what go?"

"Didn't you lead the discussion?"

"Oh, that? I thought you meant with the other kids."

"I did mean with the other kids. You can't have a discussion with one person, can you?"

"You can if you're a teacher. Don't you just love the way Jackson says we're going to discuss chapter such and such today, then he does all the talking?"

"You'd have loved O'Reilly. We spent a whole semester on Yeats, and he read every poem out loud. Actually, I think we studied every one the guy ever wrote. Too bad you weren't here sophomore year."

"Yeah. It is too bad."

The bell rang, so she didn't have to explain what she meant, which was just as well since she didn't really know. It had just popped out of her mouth before she had had a chance to censor herself.

"So where's your next class?" he asked as he picked up his lunch tray.

"Lib arts," she said, picking up her book bag and slinging it over her shoulder.

He smiled at her, picked up her tray, and slipped it under his.

"Sorry," she said embarrassed. "I'm usually not such a slob."

"And I'm usually not so neat. I was just trying to impress you."

"You did."

They walked toward the liberal arts building together, and she felt great. What an idiot she had been. It's amazing how people turn out to be their own worst enemies sometimes, she thought as they headed into the building.

"I better run," he said. "My class is across campus."

"Hurry," she said, giving him a nudge.

Chapter Eleven

Feeling light as a feather, she got off the bus and walked the four blocks to her house. The midafternoon drizzle had left a gauzelike mist that draped itself over the trees and made them look like the enchanted forest in *A Midsummer Night's Dream*. And that's the way she felt, too—enchanted. Her life had suddenly taken an unexpected turn, and the whole world looked totally different, as if it had been created just for her.

Today was Thursday. There was only Friday, Friday night, and Saturday to get through. This morning she had felt as if everything in her life was upside down. Now she felt alive and giddy with pleasure. He liked her. David liked her. And to her inordinate surprise, she liked him, too. She liked him a lot.

She walked up the driveway swinging her books. Then she stopped dead in her tracks. Her father's car was still in the garage. A bad sign. Doug's car was nowhere around. A worse sign. Either he hadn't shown up for the big confrontation yet, or he had shown up, they'd had it out, and Doug had left feeling hostile and angry. That would mean the air in the house would still be charged with tension, and everyone would have to tiptoe around her father for a few days until things cooled down.

Even if he had been wrong, and her father had, on some

level, been right, Doug wouldn't really apologize, of course. That wasn't his style. He would wait till the weekend and then do something incredibly nice like plant flowers along the front of the house without saying a word to anyone. They'd just look out and unexpectedly find them there.

She unlocked the door and walked in. The house was very quiet. Too quiet. "Mom."

No answer.

"Dad."

"We're in back," he called out.

She started walking to the bedrooms at the back of the house without even bothering to throw her books on the dining room table.

As she got closer to her parents' door, however, she heard a strange noise. She stopped and waited for a moment. Then she smiled to herself. Maybe they were taking advantage of being in the house alone on a misty afternoon.

Embarrassed for disturbing them, she was about to walk to her own room, when the soft noise coming from her parents' room became more audible. Her mother was crying. She was apparently muffling her sobs with a pillow, but the sound was unmistakable.

Shaken by the sound of her mother's sobs, Sarah returned to the front of the house and sat down at the dining room table.

She sat there for what seemed like a very long time, but she couldn't move. It was as if she had suddenly become leaden. The lightness she had felt earlier turned to stone and encapsulated her whole body. She knew it was too good to last. Something always happened to ruin things for her. Any time she felt good, any time things were really going well for her, boom, somebody would drop a bomb, and there she'd be right back on that express train to point zero. She'd take one step forward, then two steps back.

She heard her father clear his throat, then cough as he came into the room, but she didn't turn around.

"You're sitting in the dark," he said, reaching for the light switch.

The light hurt her eyes, and she winced.

"It feels better being in the dark," she said.

"I know," he sighed. "Sometimes it is better to be in the dark."

She turned and looked at him. He looked as if he'd just come back from a week's camping trip. He had a day's growth on his face. His eyes were red. His hair was in total disarray.

"Why don't you take a ride with me? I'm going to pick up some burgers for dinner."

"Hamburgers? We eating red meat again?"

"I can't think of anything else right now," he said wearily.

"Is Mom sick or something?" She couldn't remember her mother ever being too sick to make dinner. Her mother hated fast food.

"She's not feeling too well. But she'll be okay. Don't worry."

"What's wrong?" Sarah asked, though she had a very strong feeling what it was that made her mother sick enough to stay in her room crying.

When they got into the car, her father just sat there for a moment. It was as if he were in shock. He did everything in slow motion. It was creepy.

"Want me to drive?" she asked.

"What?"

"Want me to drive?"

"No. No, that's all right," he said turning on the ignition.

They drove to McDonald's in silence. After they pulled into a parking space, her father handed her a ten dollar bill and told her to get whatever she wanted.

"What do you want?" she asked.

"Doesn't matter. Whatever."

"Okay," she said, sneaking a look at him. This was really bad news, she thought. Something major took place today. Maybe things were worse than she had suspected. Maybe Doug had done something really terrible, she thought, walking into the restaurant.

He must have done something outrageous. Otherwise her father wouldn't have burned their pictures. She shivered all over again when she thought about it. That was the scariest, most bizarre thing she had ever seen in her life. What was going on?

"Next?" the girl behind the counter said. "Can I help you?"

Sarah realized she had been standing there just looking at the girl without saying anything.

She ordered quickly and stood to the side to wait for the food to come.

By the time it got there, she didn't feel much like eating either, but she picked up the bag and walked out to the car.

Her father was leaning against the steering wheel, his hands under his head. He jerked up when she opened the door.

"You're going to have to know sooner or later," he said when she got into the car.

She closed her eyes and froze, suddenly afraid to hear what her father was going to say. She wished she didn't have to hear it now. Later, she prayed. I want to put off hearing it as long as possible.

But her father didn't pay any attention to her silent prayer. He had his own agenda. He had something to tell her, and he obviously wanted to get it over with quickly.

He cleared his throat. "It's about Doug," he said, then he glanced over at her.

"That's what I figured."

"I know I scared you last night, and I'm sorry. Really sorry. That was a stupid thing to do."

That sounded pretty rational. Maybe things weren't as bad as she thought.

"Yeah. You did scare me."

"I was pretty scared myself when I realized what I was doing. I was so angry . . . I just wanted to . . . to get rid of that anger. To get rid of the person who caused that anger."

"Doug?"

"Yes."

"But those were our family pictures," she said softly.

"I know," he said, staring straight ahead even though they had stopped at a red light. "But our family is going to change a little."

"I don't understand," she said holding the warm bag as close to her body as she could."

"I . . . ah . . . I asked Douglas not to . . . not to . . . He's going to be living with a friend."

"Why?" she wailed.

"I don't want to go into that right now. Just take my word for it. It'll be better for all of us that way."

"Better for you, maybe," she yelled. "Not for Mom. I heard her. I heard her crying in your room when I got home from school. That's why she was crying, isn't it?"

"She's upset about it, but after she has a chance to think it over, I'm sure she'll realize it's for the best."

"No. No! I can't buy that. What do you mean for the best? It's not for *my* best! Not for Mom's! Not for Doug's!"

"For Doug's, too. He'll be more comfortable where he's living."

"Where? Where is he living?"

"I told you with his friend."

"*What* friend?"

"Your mother knows his name."

"My mother knows his name?"

"Yes," her father said barely moving his lips.

"I don't believe this."

"Please don't say anything to upset your mother."

"Me? As far as I can tell, she's already pretty damn upset."

"Well, don't upset her any more."

"Fine," Sarah said between clenched teeth.

When they walked into the house, her father said he'd go back and get her mother while she put some plates on the table and got drinks for them.

"What do you want to drink?" she asked as if getting the drinks would be a major chore done under extreme duress.

"Never mind," her father said. "I'll get my own drink."

"I'll get it" she said.

"I said I'd get it. I want a bourbon straight up, and I'll pour it myself, thank you."

"Thank *you*," she repeated sarcastically, under her breath, as her father walked away.

He all but commanded her mother to come to the table. Sarah could hear her protesting that she didn't want anything to eat, but her father insisted she sit down with them, anyway. To prove they were still the all-American family, no doubt. Mother, father, teenage daughter, and McDonald's. Wow! Maybe they could all say a blessing first and thank the powers that be for their good fortune.

Her mother came to the table, eyes nearly swollen shut and mouth quivering. Sarah felt sorry for her. She knew it wasn't her decision. She knew her mother had probably been up all night trying to talk her father out of his plan to wipe out her firstborn child. Because Sarah knew, in essence, that's exactly what he was doing. By forbidding Douglas to live at home, he was, in effect, wiping him out of their lives. Douglas was too proud to come back on his own, and her father was too stubborn to ever admit he had made a mistake and go after him.

They picked at their food in silence.

When her father got up to refill his drink, she leaned over to her mother and whispered, "Where is he?"

"With his friend," her mother said, barely audibly.

"What friend, for God's sake?"

"*That* friend."

"Mother!"

Her mother's chin began to quiver. She bit her bottom lip and looked away from Sarah.

"Terry?"

"Yes," her mother said still without looking at her.

"What's Terry's last name?"

"I don't know."

"Do you know his phone number, at least?" Sarah asked desperately, but she knew what her mother's answer would be.

"We don't know the phone number," her father said, walking back into the room.

"But I want to talk to him," Sarah screamed, jumping up from the table.

"It's better this way," her father said.

"Stop saying that," she screamed. "I want to see him. He's my brother."

"I'm sure he'll get in touch with us when he's ready," her mother said. Then she couldn't hold it in any longer. She began to sob.

"What? What did he do? Tell me. What could he have done that was so terrible? Did you see him sitting in the car smoking a joint or something? Wake up. Half the kids at my school smoke dope, and believe me, their parents don't kick them out of the house for it."

"I didn't see him smoking dope."

"Okay. Okay. So he was doing coke. Right? And you were really shocked. So what is he, an addict or something?"

Silence.

"If he is, we have to help him, you know. I mean, what do you want, to run into him begging at the beach or sleeping on the streets?"

"Don't be so dramatic," her father said.

"Hey, I'm just trying to find out what's going on around here," she said as tears began streaming out of her eyes. She was angry, and she was upset, and she was scared, and she was very lonely. Who were these people sitting here with her? Yesterday she had thought she knew them. She might not have loved everything about them, but at least they were familiar. But these people sitting here next to her—she had no idea where they were coming from.

The phone rang, and they all jumped, but no one made a move to answer it. Suddenly, she bolted into the kitchen and grabbed it. What if it were Doug calling to give them his number.

"Hello. Hello," she said into the receiver.

"I thought you'd forgotten to put your answering machine on again," Mrs. Collins said.

"It's on," Sarah said.

"Can I talk to your mother, dear?"

Sarah looked toward her mother who was shaking her head back and forth.

"She can't come to the phone right now. Can I take a message?"

"No, just wanted to chat. Wondered if she'd heard about Harry and Diane Dale."

"She'll call you back, Mrs. Collins," Sarah said. She hung up the phone as quickly as she could. She felt like washing the receiver afterward to get the dirt off it.

"She knows," her mother said, wailing.

"About the Dales?" Sarah asked.

"What about the Dales?" her mother asked.

"I don't know. How would I know?"

"I'll never be able to face her."

"Just tell her Douglas decided to move out and live on

his own," her father said. "She doesn't have to know anything else."

"But I do," Sarah said.

"No, you don't," her father said.

"Okay, so now you're shutting me out, too, I guess."

"We are not shutting you out," her father said wearily. "That's the last thing we want to do."

"Then tell me."

"No. I can't. I just can't tell you."

"I don't believe this. You still think I'm three years old or something. My own brother is kicked out of the house and my parents refuse to tell me why because they think I'm too stupid to handle it."

"We don't think you're stupid," her father said.

"Then naive. I am not naive. I probably know more about what goes on in this world than you do."

"Maybe you do," her father said. "Maybe you do. But I'm just not ready to talk about this yet, so you'll either have to wait until I am or hope your brother calls you so he can explain it to you."

Chapter Twelve

"I'm leaving," Sarah shouted to her parents when she heard the doorbell ring.

"Where are you going, honey?" her mother asked, sounding slightly vague. Sarah knew her mother didn't really care where she was going. She just asked out of habit. Her mother had walked around the house for the past two days looking as if she were in mourning for someone and, in a sense, she was. They all were. Only Sarah was not going to let her brother die out of the family so easily. She didn't care what he had done, or how *they* felt about him, tomorrow she would begin looking for him.

"Midnight," her father called after her as she walked to the door. She didn't even bother arguing with him. She didn't want to speak to him any more than she absolutely had to. It was his fault. He had made the decision, and her mother was too chicken to stand up to him. "I hate him," she said to herself as she opened the front door.

"Some greeting," David said. "Were you referring to me, or were you considering putting out a contract on Muladore?"

"Neither," Sarah said, embarrassed. "Though the contract isn't such a bad suggestion."

"On Muladore?"

"No."

"Want to tell me about it?" he asked, as they walked toward his car.

"Not particularly."

"So, did you decide what movie you wanted to see?"

"Anything with Sylvester Stallone," she said getting into the car.

"Sylvester Stallone. I never would have pegged you for a Stallone fan."

"I'm not. Can't stand him."

"Okay," David said as he backed out of the driveway. "I can see this is going to be an interesting evening."

"I just figured it might feel good watching someone take out his aggressions on the enemy."

"You really are mad, aren't you?"

"That's putting it mildly."

"Should we go to the Pizza Works first, or is that too tame for you?"

"It's fine."

"A sushi bar would probably be more appropriate for the mood you're in," he said, smiling at her.

"Yeah. Maybe I could get the sushi chef to let me take a few whacks at the fish, myself," she said, and she laughed. "I'm sorry. I'm being a real drag, aren't I?"

"Nah."

"Yes, I am."

"You're not."

"You're lying."

"Now you are being a drag," he teased.

"I knew it."

"Oh, come on."

"Okay. Okay. I hate sushi, anyway. I never even heard of it till we moved to L.A. Raw fish. Who wants to eat raw fish?"

Pizza Works was crowded when they got there, but they managed to squeeze into a table for two in the back, and by the time their pizza came, Sarah was feeling a little better.

"Just tell me one thing," David said before bitting into a slice of cheese pizza with the works. "You weren't talking about me, were you?"

"When?"

"When you answered the door."

"Are you crazy?"

"I didn't think so, but—"

"It's just a family problem," she sighed.

"Oh, one of those," he said, nodding his head.

"One of those."

"You can tell me about it if you want to. I'm a good listener."

"Thanks, but I'm not a very good talker," she said, retreating a little. This wasn't anything she wanted to discuss with anyone right now.

Just as she bit into her pizza, Wendy, Joni, and two guys whisked past their table and sat down at a table right next to them. Wendy spotted David first and called out to him, waving hi and making an ass out of herself in general, before she noticed Sarah. When she saw Sarah, her mouth dropped open. Wide open. And she nudged Joni, whose eyes nearly fell out of her head.

"You guys run into each other here, or what?" Wendy asked.

"Yeah, Wendy, we ran into each other," David said sarcastically.

"I was just asking," Wendy said, annoyed.

"I didn't even know you guys knew each other," Joni said.

"Lots of things you don't know," David said, teasing her.

"Guess so," Joni said.

"So how's the tennis game, Light?" one of the guys at the other table asked David.

"Great. Getting ready for the season."

Both of the guys starting talking to David, but Sarah noticed that they were also looking at her out of the corners of their eyes, not obviously or anything, just kind of sizing her up.

Wendy and Joni just kept rolling their eyes, and Sarah couldn't help smiling to herself. She knew Wendy had a crush on David. She noticed the way Wendy had looked at him when she came in. She had a big crush, so when David casually put his arm around her and asked the two guys, named Donny and Lou, if they had met Sarah yet, Sarah just beamed at all of them, thinking triumphantly to herself, eat your heart out, Wendy.

When they were about to leave, Lou, who couldn't seem to keep his eyes off Sarah, asked Sarah and David where they were going after dinner, and with a straight face, David said they were going to the Stallone film at the Coronet. He wasn't the least bit afraid of being uncool, she thought. He didn't care what they thought. She smiled, and they all smiled back at her, thinking she was smiling at them, but she was smiling at their private little joke. Hers and David's.

They left the car where it was and walked to the Coronet, not to see any violent movie, however. *My Life as a Dog* was playing there.

As they stood in line to buy the tickets, the crowd from the first show filed out, laughing and crying at the same time, talking about how terrific the movie was, and Sarah and David knew they had made the right choice.

Just as David got to the ticket line, Sarah saw Doug come out with a friend. "Doug," she shouted and broke out of the line to run after him.

He turned around when he heard his name, and the two of them raced toward each other, hugging fiercely as they clung together.

"Oh my God, why didn't you call me?" she cried. "I've been going crazy."

"I called a couple of times, but Dad answered, so I hung up," he said. "I was going to go to your school Monday to find you and tell you I was okay."

"Are you?"

"No. I don't have to now."

"I mean, are you okay?"

"Sure. Yeah. Sure I am," he said softly.

"Doug, what happened?"

"Look, we got to talk, okay? Not here. Okay?"

"Where?" she pleaded with him.

"I've been staying at my friend Terry's house for the past few days, but he and I are moving into this new place next week. I'll call you as soon as we get a phone."

"Promise?"

"Yeah, I promise."

"Got the tickets," David said, as he walked over to them, eyeing this guy with his arms around Sarah.

"Listen, I gotta run," Doug said, letting go of her. "I'm cool. I'm fine. Really. Don't worry. In a way it's the best thing."

"But I miss you."

"Me, too," he said, running off before she could even introduce him to David.

Chapter Thirteen

By the time they got back to her house, it was almost midnight. She felt a lot better going into the house than she had felt walking out of it. The movie had been fantastic. David had kept his arm around her shoulder almost the whole time, and when they had walked back to the car he had held her hand.

They had sat in the car for a long time talking about Doug, about what had happened. Actually, she had done most of the talking. David hadn't lied when he said he was a good listener, and it was a relief to talk to someone, even though she still didn't understand the actual problem any better now than she had before she ran into Doug. But at least she knew he was all right. At least she knew he had tried to get in touch with her, and she could relax a little because he had promised to call her as soon as he got a phone.

And David had said something that made a lot of sense, too. He said lots of nineteen-year-old guys move out of their parents' houses, and that because he hadn't gone off to college like most of his friends, it was probably hard on everybody. Doug was sort of an adult, but their parents still treated him like a kid because he still lived at home. After all, how many nineteen-year-olds had a curfew? There had been a lot of tension, too, even before last week, so maybe it had all just come to a head, and maybe after Doug moved into his own place everything would be all right between him and their parents again. She hoped so.

Sarah felt totally exhausted by the various emotions she had experienced all evening, and by the time she got out her key to unlock the front door, she was ready to collapse. However, when she saw there was only one small light left on in the living room, which meant her parents were already in bed, she suddenly forgot she was tired and asked David if he wanted to come in for a minute. To get a drink, or something, since he was probably thirsty from all the popcorn.

He was very thirsty, he said, as he followed her into the house. Only somehow they never made it to the kitchen to get that glass of water.

"This is a neat house," David said as he walked into the living room.

"It's okay," Sarah said.

"I like the fireplace," he said as he sat down on the back of the big, fluffy couch in front of it.

"Me, too."

"And the couch. It's so comfortable," he said, rolling over the back and onto the couch itself.

"Yeah, it is."

"Is it okay if I stretch out?"

"Sure."

He extended his long legs and totally relaxed. "God, this is more comfortable than my bed."

"I know what you mean."

"I really liked the movie."

"Me, too," she said quickly.

"You know what my favorite part was?"

"When he was boxing with the little girl?"

"Come on."

"Well, that was funny."

"Yeah, but it wasn't the funniest."

"When he tried to drink his milk, and he kept missing his mouth, and getting it all over his face?" she said, and she laughed as she remembered the scene.

"When he was up on the roof, looking in the skylight at the nude model, and he fell right through it," David said. "That was a riot."

"Oh, yeah," Sarah said, and she could feel herself blush, but she didn't exactly know why she was blushing.

"Sarah?"

"Yeah?"

"Do you want me to leave or something?"

"No? Why are you asking me that?"

"Because you're just standing there, like you're waiting for me to get up and go."

"Oh, yeah," Sarah said, and she felt as if she were in a daze.

"So why don't you sit down?"

"That's okay," she said, quickly looking around the room. She wasn't sure where she should sit. If she sat down on the couch next to him, he might think she was being very aggressive and that she was interested in—in fooling around. If she sat on the chair, she'd be too far away to really talk to him.

The chair was better, she decided, but before she could actually sit down, David was beside her. He put his arms around her and started kissing her, and before she had a chance to really think about it, she had found a place to sit down. They both had.

She'd kissed boys before. Well, she'd kissed a few of them. Friends, mostly, so she wasn't expecting the heat to rise up and surround her as it did now. Every time David backed a millimeter away, she thought she ought to tell him it was time to leave, but then he'd kiss her again, and she'd forget all about it.

This was amazing, she thought. She'd seen a million movies, but all the moaning and groaning didn't really prepare you for the real thing. Not the real thing, real thing, but the real feeling. She could go on like this for about five hours, probably more, she figured, and they hadn't even gotten around to the heavy stuff, which she wasn't really sure she was ready for quite yet. But she was ready for this. She was more than ready.

Chapter Fourteen

Sarah lay in bed trying to think about what she should be thankful for besides having a few days off from school. She knew what she wasn't thankful for. She wasn't thankful that they had been invited to the Collinses for Thanksgiving dinner, but she was thankful that they weren't going to be home alone because it was bad enough sitting down to dinner on an ordinary night. And today would be much worse than usual. She couldn't imagine a holiday without Doug. No matter how much he had fought with her parents in the past, they had never stopped talking for more than a few days, and they had never missed being together for any occasion.

Every night, ever since she had bumped into Doug outside the movie theater, she waited for him to call, but he never did, and when she had tried to locate him by calling information, she was told his number was unlisted. It had been more than a month, and she hadn't even run into him anyplace. It was as if he had dropped off the end of the earth. Maybe he was afraid to call and had sent her a letter telling her where he was, she thought, as she pulled the covers around her. Maybe her father had thrown the letter away and Doug thought she didn't care about him anymore, that she'd forgotten he existed, just as her parents seemed to have forgotten. They never talked about him. Never even mentioned his name. When Emily Collins asked how he was doing, they said, "Fine. Just fine," and changed the subject.

Still, he could have gotten to her. He could have come to school as he'd been planning to do before they ran into each other. He could have gotten in touch with her—if he had wanted to.

Had anyone asked her two months ago if she loved her brother, she wouldn't have known how to answer that question honestly. They had very little in common. Though they were only two years apart, they didn't share friends or interests. In fact, they knew very little about each other. At least she knew very little about him. Doug was quiet. He was secretive. He always had been. And she wasn't the most outgoing person in the world, either. But now that he was gone, there seemed to be a big gap in her life, and it wasn't just that she was used to seeing him around. She actually missed him. He had contributed more to the family than she realized. She missed his odd sense of humor, the way he had of seeing a funny side to even the saddest situations. She missed the way he dried the pots and pans, then slung the dish towel around his neck and tied it like an ascot. She missed the way he pretended to be Jack Nicholson doing *Hamlet*. "Ta be or not ta goddamn be . . ."

Damn, he made her mad. Where was he? This was the worst Thanksgiving of her life. Her parents couldn't even get in touch with him if they wanted to. Sarah had nothing to be thankful for today, except David. David was something she could be thankful for on this lonely Thanksgiving. They had become inseparable. Everyone called them the twins. Since they had been going out, the other kids seemed to suddenly notice that she was going to their school, too. Even Wendy and Joni stopped to talk to her when they saw her in the school cafeteria.

School—she could be somewhat thankful for that, too, she guessed. At least for art class. First of all, David was in that class, and second, she was thankful that Mrs. Bosworth had gone to substitute heaven, never to return to Longacre High, she hoped. She couldn't imagine substitutes having any kind of life outside of the classes they migrated to from day to day. She was sure they were mutants of some kind. Maybe robots that the big robot maker in the sky transformed from time to time by changing their heads, but He or She hadn't perfected the pattern yet, so they were all defective in one way or another, which was why they were still subs and not real teachers.

Mr. Hill, however, was a real teacher, and Sarah was thankful he was back. She put more and more effort into her work, and as she got more and more interested in it, he turned her on to possibilities she had never thought of. Art as a career, for example. They looked through magazines together, and he showed her ways in which design was used for products, or advertisements, or to enhance office buildings. He said artists didn't need to starve anymore. They could use their skills commercially, too, if they were interested. And he said she was good. That she was very good. That if she worked on her portfolio she could probably get into one of the better art schools after graduation. He had gone to Rhode Island School of Design himself, and he was sure he could help her get in there, if she was interested.

Rhode Island, of course, was a long way from Ohio, and her application for Ohio State sat on her desk ready to be mailed. She hadn't even written to RISD for an application yet, but the more she thought about it, the more interesting it seemed. It probably wouldn't hurt to send for some information. See what she'd be missing.

"Sarah, it's nearly noon," her father called. "Time to get up already. How about a game of tennis before we have to leave for the Collinses'?"

Sarah groaned. This was another reason why she missed Doug. A more practical one. Since he'd gone, her father seemed determined to pay as much attention to her as possible, as if it would somehow make up for Doug's not being there, or maybe help them both forget that Doug wasn't around, but she didn't want to have anything to do with him. She avoided him as much as possible.

"I'm too tired," she yelled.

"You've been in bed for twelve hours," her father said, knocking at her door.

"Okay," she groaned, giving in. She might as well. She didn't have anything else to do, and she could be with him without having to talk to him. "What time do we have to be at the Collinses'?"

"Around four."

"Who eats dinner at four?"

"It's Thanksgiving."

"I know," she grumbled. "Give me fifteen minutes."

"I'll make you some breakfast."

"I'm on a diet."

"You have to eat. I'll make some hot oatmeal with bananas and raisins and stuff in it. Delicious."

"Gruel," she mumbled as she crawled out of bed.

That was another thing. Her father had taken up cooking, too. Probably because his friend Herb Collins was a cook. She had to admit, however, it was a relief to have something besides quiche for dinner once in a while.

They played a few sets of tennis and got home just in time for her to shower and change clothes. When she walked into her room after showering, the light on her answering machine was blinking, so she rushed over to play the message, hoping David had called from Santa Barbara where he had gone to spend Thanksgiving with his grandparents. She just wanted to hear his voice. She missed him already, and she wouldn't see him until Monday morning.

She rewound the messages and turned up the volume as she rushed around the room getting her clothes together, but the minute the message began to play, she stopped what she was doing and stood holding her breath as she listened.

"Hi, kid—I know. I know. You hate me, too. It's not that I haven't been thinking about you. I have. Especially today. I thought maybe by now mom and dad and I would have patched everything up, but it doesn't look like that's going to happen. I wrote them a long letter, but the only answer I got was that they didn't want to see me. At least dad doesn't want to see me, and he wants me to stay away from you, too."

"What?" she groaned as the message played on.

"So, I figured, hell, I didn't want to get you into any kind of trouble with them, and I figured you'd be caught in the middle, which really wouldn't be fair, so I decided not to call. But I guess that's not really fair to you, either. Or to me," he said with a little, nervous laugh.

"So, if you want to get in touch with me—at least, we can talk and maybe I can explain things to you—my num—" *Click. Beep.*

"Oh my god," Sarah whispered as she rewound the message. She replayed it, listening carefully until she got to the crucial part, but the same thing happened. Doug's phone number had been cut off.

There were two other families already at the Collinses' when they got there, and she could see right away that her mother was terribly embarrassed. Not because of her dessert—she had brought a pumpkin pie and a gorgeous-looking apple pie—but because of what she was wearing. The other women all had on handmade, oversized sweaters, tight leggings, and boots. At first they were indistinguishable from their daughters. Her mother had dressed as she always did for important holidays, in a dress. A perfectly nice dress. In fact she looked terrific. Better than she had since Doug left.

Sarah hadn't mentioned anything to her parents about his call, but she was determined to get his address from them as soon as they got home from this nightmare dinner.

Emily hugged and kissed them all as if they hadn't seen one another for weeks, though she had just been at their house yesterday. Donna Alexander rushed into the kitchen with the apple pie, and Sarah followed her carrying the pumpkin. As soon as she put the apple pie down on the kitchen counter, her mother burst into tears, leaving both Sarah and Emily, who had also come into the room, speechless.

Finally, Emily, who usually couldn't go for more than two minutes without talking, found her voice and asked, "What is it, Donna? What happened?"

Her mother just shook her head and refused to answer. Emily inspected the pies. "They look great," she said. "Nothing happened to the pies, did it?"

Her mother shook her head no.

"Aw, I know," Emily said, putting her arms around Donna. "You wish Doug hadn't gone skiing for the weekend, don't you?"

Her mother nodded her head yes, and tried to wipe away her tears without ruining her mascara.

"Well, I can understand that," Emily said. "I feel the same way when Wendy's with her father and not with me, but thing is, hon, you just have to learn to let go, if you know what I mean."

Sarah wanted to confront her mother right there and ask her how she could have known Doug had gone skiing if she hadn't spoken to him for weeks, but she decided to drop it. It wasn't any of Emily's business, anyway.

"I love that outfit," Emily said. "Glen plaid is so in this season."

"It is?" her mother asked like a little kid who's too insecure to know if she's really made a good mud pie.

"I like the length, too. Wish I'd have worn my beige,"

Emily said, biting her bottom lip. "Wonder if I should go up and change. No—that would be too much, wouldn't it?"

Sarah couldn't believe this conversation. Not even the girls at Longacre would go up and change their clothes if they thought someone else was dressed better than they were—no matter how much they might want to.

Her mother seemed to regain her equilibrium, and the three of them walked back into the living room where everyone else was either watching the football game or comparing notes on what was in and what was out. Sarah was surprised to hear that ponytails for men were now in, and Cajun cooking was out. She smiled as she thought of David, who was in even though he hadn't meant to be, but she had no idea that Cajun cooking had been in, so she sure as hell was surprised to learn that it was out now. In fact, she didn't even know what Cajun cooking was.

Wendy and her stepsister Joni tried to engage Sarah in conversation asking her how school was going and how she liked living in California, but Sarah had trouble paying attention to what they were saying. She kept glancing over at her mother, worried she might suddenly burst into tears again. Her father seemed to be belting down more than usual, and though he was always friendly and liked to joke around at parties, she thought he was getting a little out of control and hoped they'd sit down to dinner soon.

Wendy and Joni invited her to come up to the bedroom they shared on weekends and holidays when Joni was staying with her father, but Sarah was reluctant to go. They insisted, however, all but dragging her away from the adults.

As soon as they got to the room, they collapsed on the bed in torrents of giggles and reached for the tightly rolled cigarettes hidden in a drawer of the nightstand. Wendy lit one, inhaled deeply, and passed it on to Joni. She took a long drag, then handed it to Sarah. Sarah paused for a moment, then handed it back to Wendy. Wendy and Joni exchanged glances and Sarah sensed that the wall they had torn down was being rebuilt, but she just smiled at both of them and realized she didn't need or even want to be accepted by either Wendy or Joni.

She sat down on the bed next to them and relaxed. She had nothing to lose here. They liked her, or they didn't. Either way it was all right with her.

She looked around the room. Shopping bags from Guess, Jess, The Limited, and Esprit covered the walls like prized paintings. On the walls of Sarah's bedroom were reproductions of a Cezanne, a Picasso, a Miró print, and a few of her own paintings. Some day, when she had money of her own, she hoped to replace the reproductions with originals. Maybe not Picassos or Cezannes or Mirós, but possibly works of a few young painters who would someday be famous, too.

When Emily called to them announcing the buffet had been set up and the turkey was ready to be carved, Sarah was relieved. She hoped they could eat quickly and get out of there as soon as possible after dinner, so she could confront her parents and get Doug's address, but she knew her parents would stay and stay and stay until most of the others had gone, and she'd be forced to either try to fade into the woodwork or join the others and answer their inane questions.

They all piled their plates high with turkey, stuffing, cranberry mold, and broccoli and sat down to stuff themselves. Herb Collins poured wine into each of their glasses and said that even the kids could have a sniff if they wanted to. Sarah laughed to herself. What the hell did he think they did when he wasn't around? She'd heard about a party recently where Wendy had belted down a six pack of beer, but now she was pretending half a glass of wine was way too much for her.

Sarah spaced out during the meal and let the conversation

just float around her. Every now and then she'd look up and smile, and someone would smile back at her. Then the weirdest thing happened. Andrea Peters, a friend of Emily's, said she'd heard a rumor about one of the teachers at Longacre. Sarah perked up, wondering what she'd heard. When Mrs. Peters mentioned Mr. Hill's name, Sarah's mind jumped to attention.

"Well, I don't like to say," Andrea said coyly. "After all, it is just a rumor."

"Well, for God's sake, pass it on," Emily said.

"He's pregnant," Sarah's father said, pleased with his little joke.

"That should only be the case," Andrea said.

"What is it, then?" Constance Alter asked.

Andrea looked around at Sarah, Wendy, Joni, and the other teenagers sitting at the table. "I don't think I should say anything in front of the kids. After all, one of them might know him."

"They don't know him," Emily said impatiently.

"Just drop it, Andrea," Mr. Peters said. "Why do you want to start anything?"

"I'm not the one who started it," Andrea Peters said in a huff.

"But you're the one who wants to pass it on, and we have no real evidence that it's true."

"Well, what if we did?" Mrs. Peters asked.

"If we did, damn it, we'd have to do something about it. You know how I feel about that issue."

Sarah didn't know what Mr. Peters was talking about, and evidently no one else at the table did either.

"Flora D'Angelo ought to know," Andrea said.

"Flora D'Angelo?" Emily said. "Isn't she that friend of yours who's a nurse?"

"Exactly," Andrea said, with a smirk.

Sarah's stomach lurched. Somehow it signaled to her that

something was very wrong, but her head couldn't quite
connect with what it might be.

"Andrea," Mr. Peters warned.

"You can't start something, then just drop it," Emily
said, leaning in toward Andrea. "We can keep a secret."

"Well, as I said, we have no real verification about this.
We just heard about it this morning, in fact, when Flora
called to wish us a happy Thanksgiving, and she doesn't
even have the information firsthand, but right after the holiday, John is going directly to school to ask Ms. McAllister
just what she knows about this matter."

"So I suggest we just wait until Monday before we say
any more," John Peters said.

"We're all friends here," Emily said. "Go on, tell us."

Sarah knew Mrs. Peters wouldn't be able to keep the
secret, whatever it was, but she was beginning to feel sick
to her stomach. She hated the way they were all sitting here
talking about Mr. Hill as if he had committed some terrible
crime or something. And to make matters worse, they didn't
even know the man. None of them knew him except her.
Her parents had never even met him, though they knew she
was in his class. They weren't saying anything, however.
Maybe they were afraid she'd be guilty by association if
they admitted that she was in his class.

"Well," Mrs. Peters said. "Flora said that he has *that*
disease."

"*That* disease?" Emily asked confused.

"You know what I mean," Andrea said emphatically.

"I have no idea what you mean," Emily said.

"*It.* He has *it.*"

"Can you believe this? The woman can't even say it,"
Emily said laughing.

"A-I-D-S," Andrea Peters spelled out. "The man has
AIDS."

Everyone at the table stopped eating and stared at Mrs.
Peters.

"You'd better be very sure before you pass on a thing like that," Sarah's father said after a few moments.

"Exactly what I said," Mr. Peters mumbled.

"But if he does—if the man has it, then we've got to get him out of the school—and fast!" Sarah's father said emphatically, as he pushed his chair back and got up from the table.

Chapter Fifteen

Sarah sat through Mr. Hill's class just staring at her paints. She felt as if she had lost control of her life. When she had first asked, then demanded Doug's address after they returned from the Collinses', her parents had thrown total fits. Her mother, who had obviously known nothing about the letter until Sarah had asked about it, flew into her room in tears, and her father, whose face was beet red with anger, spat out, "I don't have his damn address. Did you think I'd keep the damn letter around the house?" Then he had stormed out of the house, slamming the door behind him. So her art seemed so pointless now. How could she work on expressing herself when all she felt was anger and frustration? She knew what was going on in the principal's office that very moment. She knew because her father and Mr. Collins were in there with Ms. McAllister, and she knew exactly what they were planning to discuss. She hoped and prayed it wasn't true. That there was no reason to fire him.

She glanced up at him and winced. He looked better than he had when he came back to school after his bout in the hospital, but he was so thin.

David hadn't returned from his grandmother's in time to call her last night, so she hadn't spoken with him since

Wednesday. He was standing in his usual place at the back of the classroom, looking at her, probably wondering why she wasn't working. He worried about her. She liked that. Even though she didn't like seeing him worried. She could hardly wait till class was over so they could talk. At the same time she wasn't sure she wanted to admit she knew Mr. Hill was in trouble, and that her father was one of the people causing the trouble. She was afraid it would not only hurt Mr. Hill, but hurt her as well. What would David think? Would he blame her for what her father was doing?

She glanced at her watch. Twenty-five more minutes.

"Listen, kids," Mr. Hill said quietly. "Could you start cleaning up?"

Jimmy looked at the wall clock. "We got twenty-five more minutes, man."

"I know."

"We don't usually clean up till ten to."

"I'd like to talk to you about something, and I'd kind of like your attention," Mr. Hill said, smiling at them.

"Oh boy, surprise," Bobby said. "I can feel it in the air."

"We takin' another field trip, Mr. Hill?" Nick asked.

"Nope."

"Too bad. That was the first time I ever had a legitimate reason for cutting my morning classes," Bobby said laughing.

Sarah finished cleaning up first, because all she had to do was put her painting in the back of the room against the wall where they were stored until they were finished and dry.

When she walked to the back of the room, she passed David's area and stopped for a moment. She wanted to say something right then, but she couldn't. Her throat was totally dry, and her head felt as if it had been attached to someone else's body. So instead she just smiled rather weakly and mouthed, "Glad you're back."

"Okay, Hill, babe, we are at your service," Bobby said after a few minutes. "Everybody is dying to hear the big surprise."

Mr. Hill cleared his throat. "I've been thinking about this all weekend," he began. "At first I had decided not to say anything to anybody. I felt that it wouldn't be appropriate, but this morning Ms. McAllister informed me that two of the parents were coming to talk to her about me, and I knew at that moment I would have to talk to my classes."

"Hill, babe, tell us who they are, man, we'll break their kneecaps for you."

"Thanks, Bobby, I appreciate your vote of confidence, but maybe you'd better hold off a minute till I finish."

"I like this class," Jimmy said. "I didn't think I would, but I like it. It's cool. What kind of moron would complain about it, anyway?"

"Hey, Hill," Nick called out. "This is the only class worth anything in this school. Don't let anyone tell you nothing different, man."

"Yeah," Bobby agreed. "That's pretty true."

"So what's the problem, anyway?" Jimmy asked. "They heard the rumor going around school or something?"

"You know?" Mr. Hill asked, leaning forward in utter shock.

"Sure," Jimmy said. "We all know. Right, guys?" he asked, winking at Sarah.

Sarah knew what he was referring to and went into shock herself. How could she stop this?

"You know?" Mr. Hill asked again.

"We know," Bobby said. "Big deal. What do you think we are? A bunch of babies, or something. Think we can't handle something like that?"

"Well, I must admit, I am a bit surprised at your attitude—and very delighted," Mr. Hill said. "I wanted to tell you before it got around the school. I just thought it was only fair that my students hear about it from me first rather than someone else," he said, and Sarah could see his whole body relax. She realized just how nervous he was about talking to them. She wished she could warn him before he went any further, but she sat there, horrified, unable to stop the fiasco she knew was bound to occur.

"Hill, you're making a mountain out of a mole hill," Nick said. "We are seniors in high school. We been around, you know."

"Lots of people have been around," Mr. Hill said, "but that doesn't stop them from being totally freaked out by AIDS."

A profound and stunning silence filled the room. Jimmy, Nick, and Bobby literally sat in their seats with their mouths hanging open. Sarah couldn't see anyone else without turning her head, and at that moment, she was frozen in time and space staring directly at Mr. Hill so that she saw him totally deflate when Bobby said, "Aren't you talkin' about the nude model, man?"

Chapter Sixteen

Sarah heard a deep groan as if it had come from the bottom of someone's heart. It wasn't until she felt everyone's eyes on her that she realized the groan had come from her. She wanted to yell at them. She wanted to tell them to stop looking at her. She wanted to tell them to close their mouths and just go on with their lives. To forget what Mr. Hill had just said. She knew that AIDS was a killer. She remembered that from the articles she'd read. And she knew that babies whose mothers had AIDS were often born infected with the disease. She knew about hemophiliacs with AIDS. There was a TV movie about a boy who had become infected through a transfusion. She knew about drug users who got AIDS from sharing needles. But it didn't kill your normal, average high school kids. Did it? She didn't actually know any kids who had died of it, and she was sure, knowing Mr. Hill as she did, he would never do anything to jeopardize his students. From what she could remember, AIDS was transmitted by sexual contact, not by breathing on someone.

She looked up at him. He looked as if he would faint right there in the classroom. Why couldn't she reach out to him? Why couldn't any of them? How could they just sit there in silence?

Finally, Mr. Hill pulled himself together and announced that class was dismissed, even though they still had five minutes to go. Before anyone could scramble for the door, however, he hurried out himself, leaving them behind.

No one moved for a moment, then Bobby jumped out of his seat. "I ain't comin' back here," he said under his breath. "No way."

"Me neither," Jimmy said, shaking his head.

"Think he's gonna die?" Nick asked.

"We all die, dummy," Bobby said.

"I mean like soon, man."

"Of course, he's gonna die. Didn't you see that show on TV?" Jimmy said. "If you have AIDS, you die."

"I'm getting out of here," Tom said, rushing for the door. "This whole damn place is probably contaminated."

"My old man is gonna freak out," Bobby said. "He didn't want me in any pansy art class in the first place."

"Hey, you guys, this is making me really nervous," Jeffrey said, looking as if he were about to wet his pants. "Do you think we're all gonna get it?"

"He comes around and touches our stuff," Bobby said cringing. "He walks around the room and breathes all over us."

"Jesus," Jimmy said. "We're all gonna die."

"Once he sneezed when he was right in front of me," Nick said, covering his own mouth as if he could protect himself now.

"He's queer," Jimmy said suddenly. "Either that or he's shooting up heroin, and I ain't seen any track marks on his arms. That's how you get it. I seen that on the show."

"He keeps his arms covered," Bobby said. "Maybe he's not queer."

"I don't care if he is, or isn't. Or if he shoots up every damn time he leaves the room," Nick said. "He has it. Right? He said he had it. It ain't no rumor. He said it himself. So I, for one, do not plan on coming into this room again until they get rid of Hill and spray it with disinfectant.''

"I think we could sue the school. That's what I think," Bobby said.

"What do you mean, 'sue the school'?" Jimmy asked.

" 'Cause they should protect us. That's their job, isn't it?''

"Yeah. I think we *should* sue the school," Nick said.

"Why the hell are we just sitting here like idiots? Let's get out of here, you guys," Bobby said as he headed for the door.

"Could I say something?" David asked calmly.

"Outside," Bobby said. "Say it outside in the fresh air."

"No. You've been in here for weeks. Nothing is going to happen to you if it hasn't happened already. This is between us. Between the kids in our class right now. There's no reason to spread it around the school."

"Okay. Okay, but talk fast," Nick said nervously as he paced the room.

"You don't catch AIDS by being in the same room with a person who has it," David said.

"Oh yeah, and how do you know that?" Jimmy said.

"Trust me. I know," David said.

"Oh yeah, wise guy, well I know that it's highly contamible, or whatever," Bobby said.

"Communicable," David said. "Yeah, it is, but as far as I know none of us has shared a needle with Mr. Hill or has had sex with him."

"What are you crazy, man!" Bobby said rushing over to David. "You calling me a fag, or something?"

"Just the opposite. I know you're not. And you're not a drug addict, either, so I presume you've never gotten that close to Mr. Hill. Right?"

"Not *that* close, moron, but the guy breathes all over me."

"You can't get AIDS from someone's breath."

"How come you know so much about it, man?" Jimmy asked, suspiciously.

"From my father."

"From your old man?" Bobby asked shocked.

"Your old man has AIDS?"

Sarah froze. She remembered the time she had met David in Ms. Colburn's class after school. He had said he was going to the hospital to see his father. If his father had AIDS, David could have it. They had drunk out of the same glass. Shared candy and stuff. Though he had walked to the front of the room when he started talking, she couldn't bear to look at him. She couldn't stand for him to see how scared she was herself. Not about being in the same room with Mr. Hill, but about being with David. Kissing him. Suddenly, the feel of his mouth on hers, the gentle searching of his tongue, made her sick to her stomach. She hated him for not telling her, for exposing her to . . . death.

"My father is a doctor," David said.

"He get it from a patient?" Jimmy asked horrified.

"He doesn't have AIDS."

"Man, you really had me scared there for a minute," Bobby said.

Sarah started to breathe again.

"He's doing research on AIDS," David said. "He's trying to come up with a vaccine of some kind so people will stop dying from this plague."

"Plague?"

"Well, it is a plague in a way because it's spreading so fast, and so many people have already died from it."

"And you want us to just sit here and say, okay, so Hill has it, but we're gonna just stick around to let him know we trust him not to give it to us?" Bobby asked.

"More or less," David said. "He needs our support. Things are gonna be pretty rough for him in the next few days, I think. If some of the parents have already gone to

McAllister to complain, that means the crap is gonna hit the fan pretty soon."

"I don't know," Nick said. "I don't know. Are you sure we can't get it from him?"

"You could get it from him, Nick, you queer," Jimmy said derisively.

"I never did it with *him*," Nick said defensively.

"Look, you guys, I swear to God, you can't get it from someone if they breathe on you or cough, or anything like that. You can't get it by casual contact. My dad's said that a million times to my mom 'cause she was worried about it, too, especially because he's working on it. But he knows enough to take precautions when he does their blood work."

"I saw this guy on 'Nightline' who got AIDS. This doctor who got it from somebody else's blood," Bobby said.

"Yeah, I know about that. That's pretty bad," David said. "He did get it from a patient's blood. The test tube broke in his hands, he wasn't wearing gloves, and he had a cut, so his blood was in direct contact with the patient's."

"So, see," Bobby yelled. "He didn't screw the guy. He didn't share a needle with him, and he got it anyway."

"From the guy's blood," David said. "How many times has Hill bled all over you?"

"Well, what if he does? What are we supposed to do? Wear rubber gloves in here all the time?"

"Look, the AIDS virus is very, very fragile. It doesn't live for more than a few seconds after it hits the air."

"Virus!" Jimmy yelled. "Viruses are right up there, in the air. People get viruses all the time," he said, panicked.

"Those viruses *can* be caught by casual contact," David explained patiently, but by now most of the guys were too panicked to listen.

"I don't want to die, man. That's all there is to it," Bobby said, finally. "I just don't want to die, and if there's any chance—any chance at all that I could get AIDS from

Hill, then the hell with his feelings. If he hadn't been a queer, he wouldn't have gotten it, either.''

"You don't have to be gay to get it," David said.

"A druggie, then," Bobby said.

"There are babies who are born with it."

"What?"

"Yeah. Babies. Because their mothers are infected. And kids, little kids, because they've had blood transfusions, and the blood they got was contaminated."

"What is this? The whole damn country's got it?" Jimmy asked, angrily.

"No, but a lot of people do," David said.

"And, like I said, I don't want to be one of them," Bobby shouted, "so I'm outta here. Hill will have to fight his battles without me."

"Wait," David called after him as Bobby walked out of the room.

"You wait," Bobby called back. "You be a jerk if you want to. I ain't taking any more chances."

Bobby slammed the door leaving a trail of fear and hostility behind him. The rest of the class got up and shuffled out after him.

Chapter Seventeen

"Let's go," David said as he walked over to Sarah's desk.

She wasn't ready to move yet. She felt fogged over with too much information thrown at her too fast. Too many mixed feelings were assaulting her from every direction. She was both relieved and frightened, angry and upset, proud of David and annoyed that once again, he had to be different from everyone else. She wanted to believe he was right. She had to believe it, not only because she loved and trusted him, but because she felt Mr. Hill had already suffered enough. She didn't want him to have to face any more indignities. But if she loved David, if she believed in him, what did that say about her father? Did it mean she would have to reject him, reject what he believed? She wished she could remember what she had read in all those articles. She wished she had paid more attention during the discussion, which she herself had led, but it just hadn't seemed relevant then. It hadn't seemed like anything she'd ever have to think about again, so she had dismissed it from her mind as soon as the test was over.

"We've already missed most of lunch," he said, pulling her up from her seat.

"Who cares about eating."

"I do."

"How can you?"

"Life goes on. We have to do what we can do," he said. "We have to try to teach people the difference between fact and fiction, but we can't do that if we're hungry," he said, smiling at her.

"You're so . . . so . . . I don't know. You're just so calm," she said bitterly. He was so different from her father. He just didn't fit into any mold. Why didn't he just scream and shout at everyone in the class, tell them they were crazy—or stupid—or something? Why did he have to logically try to explain everything as if people listened to logic? They didn't. They listened to emotion. They paid attention to the most flamboyant speakers, the ones who used catch phrases people could remember and pass on. Logic had nothing to do with it. The guys in the class wouldn't remember that David had told them you couldn't catch AIDS by casual contact. They would remember that he had called AIDS a plague. That had hit them right in the middle of their emotional baggage, and everything he had said after that just didn't count.

"I'm only calm on the outside," he said looking into her eyes. "On the inside I'm just as scared as everyone else."

"You?"

"Maybe more so."

"But you don't seem to care what anybody else thinks."

"I do, and I don't. I care enough to want people to like me, listen to me, but not enough to change who I am to get them to do that."

She melted. She loved this guy. And she trusted him. In spite of her doubts, of her fears, she knew on a deeper level that he was right. What she wasn't sure of was her ability to defend him or, for that matter, to defend Mr. Hill who was much more vulnerable than David.

He put his arm around her, and they walked to the door. Before he opened it, however, he turned to her and kissed her lightly at first, then more deeply, his arms tightening around her so that she felt his strength and his energy, and she knew she would stand by him no matter what. He kissed her again and again, and she kissed him back, moving her hands under his shirt, caressing his back. His own hands moved over her body as they pressed against the wall breathing together, grasping for each other, their mouths soft with the pressure of each other's lips.

She wanted it to go on and on. She wanted to tear off his clothes and bite him softly all over his body. She wanted him to touch her in places where she'd barely touched herself. She completely forgot they were in school, in a classroom, standing next to a door that anyone could open at any moment.

The bell announcing the end of lunch period startled them both and they jumped apart. She was shaking. She wasn't ready to leave. She looked at David. They were both breathing hard, their faces were flushed, and their bodies were warm. This was love, she thought. This was like and lust combined. And that, she decided right then and there, was what love was—like and lust combined. She wasn't just in lust. She was in love.

"Some things are more important than lunch," David said as he touched her face gently.

They both put themselves back together as well as they could and walked out of the room together.

"Maybe we should cut out of here and go to my house," he said without looking directly at her. "Get some lunch," he added quickly. "My mom drove to UCLA with my dad today, so I have her car."

"Okay," she said, barely breathing.

"I think I can put together a couple of sandwiches without too many problems," he said a little nervously, as they walked out of the building and toward the car. Even though they were inseparable, they'd never really been *alone* in either of their houses before.

"Are you allowed to have kids over when your parents

aren't home?'' she asked as they pulled out of the parking lot.

"Why not?"

"I'm not allowed to."

"My parents told my brother and me the same thing. The house is yours as well as ours. As long as you respect our needs, we'll respect yours."

"Pretty broad minded," she said, laughing.

"Yeah, well, sounds better than it is in real life. I mean, it works okay with me because I pretty much believe in the same things my parents do, and I don't do drugs, or . . . or bring girls home, or anything. At least, I never did before," he added. "But I know they wouldn't care," he said quickly, "and even if they did, they wouldn't care once they knew how I felt about you."

"Which is?"she asked in a whisper.

"I think you know," he said.

"I know how your body feels," she said. "I'm asking about your brain right now."

"They agree," he laughed, but he just couldn't make himself say what she wanted to hear. It was too scary.

When they pulled into the driveway of David's house, he swore under his breath as he parked behind an old green Ford.

"I guess somebody's home, after all," she said, and she was both disappointed and relieved. As much as she wanted David, she wasn't sure she was ready to go that one extra step just yet. "Do you have a housekeeper?"

"It's not the housekeeper's car," he said as he opened the car door. "If he's in his room, we'll grab something to eat and leave. If he's in the kitchen, we'll just smile and walk out the back door."

"Your father?"

"My brother."

"Won't he think something's weird if we just walk in one door and out of another?" she asked, wondering what this brother she'd only heard about, but had never met, was really like.

"My brother doesn't think anything's weird, that is, if he thinks at all."

"So this is where your parents' philosophy breaks down, huh?"

"I keep thinking my mother must have been impregnated by some creature from outer space," he said. "He doesn't even look like anyone in our family."

"I can't wait to meet him."

"Believe me, you'll be sorry once you do."

David unlocked the front door of the large, two-story house that reminded Sarah of the house back home—in Ohio. It was red brick, not stucco like most of the other houses in Longacre, and there were leaves falling from the maple trees outside. All the trees on her block were palms. The smell of autumn was in the air here, and she realized how tired she was of the unrelenting good cheer of summer. Without knowing exactly why, she felt comfortably at home here.

"Just don't go into cardiac arrest if you see him," he said as he led her toward the kitchen.

Sarah barely had time to take in the large airy room, gleaming white without being antiseptic. The smell of something wonderful filled the air, and she realized there was soup cooking on the stove. How bad could this brother be? He cooked, and he obviously cleaned up after himself.

"My mom must have put up some soup before she left for school this morning," David said. "She doesn't have to be at UCLA until eleven on Mondays."

As he opened the refrigerator, what could only have been David's brother emerged from a john next to the kitchen, and Sarah almost gasped.

Leering at her was a guy with bright orange hair, a color she couldn't have duplicated on her palette, no matter how hard she tried. He was wearing a gray suede vest with fringe hanging from it, and an ornate gold cross was dangling from his chest. He wore nothing else on top. Covering his legs were jeans so old and torn, she wasn't quite sure how he kept them on. On his right ear was an earring with a spiked cross, and through his nose was a small gold hoop. His feet were shoved into an old pair of black cowboy boots with spurs clanking on the backs.

He took off his dark sunglasses when he spotted her and just stood there and smiled audaciously.

"Whoa," he said. "If it isn't the princess and the pea."

"Hi, Mark," David said.

"Pea brain, I told you to call me Zed, didn't I?"

"Sorry. I keep forgetting."

"And who, may I ask, is your friend?"

"You may not ask, and we're just leaving."

"But you just came."

"Right."

"Aw, I know. Davie, Davie," he said, pointing his finger at David and laughing. "Mommy and Daddy wouldn't like to come home and find you know who, doing you know what, you know where. Would they now?"

"We just came to grab something to eat," David said defensively.

"Well, then, be my guest," Mark said, opening the refrigerator door that David had slammed shut when Mark had walked into the room.

"I already looked. Nothing there," David said, walking past Mark.

Mark grabbed him and squeezed his arm tightly. "I don't think you looked hard enough, pal. There's plenty to eat in there. Always is," he added more calmly as he let go of David's arm.

"Look, Mark—Zed—this was really a bad idea. We're going to be late for class."

"Hey, you don't have to make up any excuses. This is your house. You come and go as you like. Right? We all

come and go as we like. Only some of us like to go a little
more than others and like to stay away a little longer. Sorry
I spoiled your fun, Davie boy. To tell you the truth I was
beginning to wonder if you were normal. Glad to see you
have the same drives as the rest of us," he said reaching
into his pocket.

"Shut up," David said. "Just shut up."

"Cool out, man," Mark said, flipping something to
David he had taken out of his pocket. "I'm outta here.
You're on your own. Unless you need some pointers, of
course," he said, laughing at his own joke as he opened the
back door and exited.

Sarah just stood there, looking at David. She was wrong.
There was something that could shake him up, and that
something obviously was his brother. She could understand
why. Just looking at this kid was enough to make a person
cross the street and walk in the other direction.

"I see what you mean," she said finally.

"What?"

"About the creature from outer space."

"Yeah," David said wearily, still clutching whatever it
was Mark had thrown him.

"What's his story?"

"It would take too long to explain."

"How much older is he than you?"

"Two years younger."

"He's only sixteen?"

"He's been around."

"I thought he was at least twenty."

"So does he."

"He goes to Longacre?"

"Did. He dropped out."

"Your parents let him?"

"They had no choice. He was too strung out to go back
to school this semester. They told him he had to get it
together, stop using drugs, and clean up his act before

Christmas, or they were going to put him into the hospital.''

"Has he?''

"No.''

"It's almost Christmas.''

"Right.''

"So what's going to happen?''

"I don't know. They're really upset . . . for a lot of reasons. Mostly, they're scared. They've been going to meetings. We all have. They told him either he goes into the hospital voluntarily, or they commit him if he's still using in two weeks.''

"Some people lock their kids out of the house—''

"Yeah, some people do, but not my parents. They wouldn't do that, and as much as I want to choke him sometimes for being so stupid, I wouldn't want them to, either. He's just a kid. A stupid kid, but he's my brother, so we do what we can do, and we hope he'll come around eventually.''

"What'd he throw you?''

"Nothing,'' David said, blushing.

"What? Come on. I'm curious.''

David opened his hand and revealed a condom. Sarah blushed, too, sorry she had insisted on his showing her what he was holding.

"Guess he's not that stupid,'' David said. "At least he's smart enough to use clean needles. My father drummed that into his head, and it looks like he's smart enough to use condoms, too. Anybody who doesn't is not only stupid, but crazy.''

"You mean 'cause he . . . he does it with girls he doesn't know very well?''

"I mean because he wears a condom no matter how well he knows a girl. He might know her, but he sure as hell doesn't know all the guys she might have slept with.''

"We better get going,'' Sarah said, a little uncomfortable with the turn in the conversation.

"Sarah," David said softly, obviously feeling more like his old self again, "Sarah, I'm sorry my brother ruined it for us."

"I'm sorry, too," she whispered.

He put his arms around her again and began stroking her hair, but this was not the time. Both of them had too many things to think about, and they were both very much aware that Mark had a key to the house and could walk in the door any time he pleased. After all, as David said, the house was his, too.

Well, she thought ironically, the threat of Mark's bursting in on them was even better protection than the protection he had thrown to David.

Chapter Eighteen

Sarah's life was a strange mixture of joy and sorrow. She and David were together constantly, and together they had tried to track down Doug, but they couldn't find him, and he had never called her again. She was sure Doug thought she didn't want to get involved in his problems, get in the middle of the "situation" between him and their father.

By this time both sets of parents knew how Sarah and David felt about each other. What they didn't know was that, while Sarah's family was busily campaigning to remove Mr. Hill from his classes, David's family was putting pressure on the school board to retain him. She and David decided it would be better to keep both sets of parents in the dark, though Sarah suspected David's parents would be much more tolerant of her parents' view than her parents would be of his.

There had been one really close call when her father, going through a list of parents he wanted to contact to speak at the board meeting, said he was going to call David's father because he was a doctor and could tell everyone once and for all just how deadly this disease was.

Sarah had talked him out of it, saying that he was very shy and would never speak in front of a group of people, so her father had gotten someone else instead.

What neither Sarah nor David had counted on, however,

was just how passionately involved both their fathers would become in the issue. They each planned to speak at the emergency board meeting that evening. Mr. Alexander to oust Mr. Hill, and Dr. Light to retain him.

When they got to the school auditorium that evening, it was so packed that the meeting had to be moved to the Civic Center next to City Hall to accommodate everyone.

Sarah came with her parents, and David came with his. They looked at each other longingly, intentionally separated by rows of indignant parents. They didn't want their families anywhere near each other.

Catherine Willett, chairman of the school board, called the meeting to order, and they went over the old business first just as if this were an ordinary Thursday night and everyone had all the time in the world.

Finally, one of the board members moved that because so many people had signed up to speak, perhaps they should table any remaining discussion and get right to the issue for which most of the audience had come.

Mrs. Willett called for a show of hands and saw that everyone agreed, so she proceeded by saying that she would call people to speak in the order in which they had signed up. Since there were so many who wanted to express their opinions, she hoped they would be brief so they could adjourn the meeting by eleven. In fact, to assure brevity, she was going to impose a two-minute limit on each speaker, and at the end of that time Mr. Simon would ask the speaker to wind up his or her comments and sit down. She also added that she hoped people would pass when it came to them if they had already heard their comments stated by someone else.

Fat chance, Sarah thought. She'd listened to her parents and their friends go over this for the past week. They kept repeating themselves over and over again, but they all insisted on being heard, and they all wanted to make sure everyone else knew exactly how they each felt.

Several people went up to the podium, shuffled their papers, and made rather inane comments either for or against Mr. Hill. The audience was beginning to get bored. People began talking to each other instead of listening to the speakers. Some were even moving around the auditorium either polling whether people were for or against Hill, or socializing. So far no one had said anything either very convincing or very moving.

"Mr. Roger Alexander," Mrs. Willett said into the mike.

Sarah's father jumped out of his seat and headed for the front of the auditorium. Sarah shrank down as far as she could and hoped David's parents wouldn't think she felt the same way her father did. She also hoped he'd just say it and get it over with without any dramatics.

"My name is Roger Alexander. My family and I moved to Longacre in June. The reason we chose this community was because it's so all-American, and I mean that in the best sense. This community embodies all the things people strive for—good government, good public facilities, good internal transportation, good health facilities, and most important of all, good schools. That good school system was the main reason we chose to live here, and quite frankly, we think we made the right choice. We still think so despite the problem that has recently arisen, because we know that in this democratic community where people can be heard, where their opinions are taken seriously, this school board will listen and learn and understand that we have every right to protect ourselves, to, in fact, protect the American way of life.

"Now I feel for Craig Hill. Believe me, I'm no ogre. I think the man has suffered a great deal already, and I'm in favor of helping him maintain in any way he can. In fact, I'd like to start a fund just for that purpose, but I cannot stand here and let him teach in my child's school, in the classroom in which she sits every day of the week."

Sarah shrank down even further and tried to disappear. She felt her mother hanging on her father's every word, and she wanted to scream.

"We're all bright people," her father went on. "Bright enough to realize doctors aren't gods. Sure, they've told us we can't catch AIDS from casual contact, but let's look at what else they've said. They've contradicted themselves over and over again. Most researchers say AIDS is caused by the HIV virus, but there are dissenters who point out that the virus isn't found in all of the patients who have died of the disease. In fact, according to a Dr. Duesberg's interpretation of the literature on AIDS, the virus has been found in only fifty percent of AIDS patients. Only antibodies to the virus have been found in virtually all those with the disease. So who's right? Does the HIV virus cause AIDS, or doesn't it? There was a time when medical researchers suspected that other viruses might also be responsible. Question is—why'd they change their minds? Because they were pressured into it? Maybe it's true that the HIV virus can't be transmitted by casual contact, but what if other viruses also cause AIDS? And what if they can be transmitted just like the flu or the common cold? That's the big question."

Sarah looked around her. People were beginning to nod their heads in agreement with her father, and she had to admit, though she tried to resist, she was beginning to be a little swayed herself.

"Today they tell us you can't catch AIDS by casual contact, but what will doctors tell us tomorrow? And what about the doctors who refuse to treat AIDS patients? Oh—sure—I know they have to adhere to the Hippocratic oath and treat everyone who comes in for help, but you and I know there are ways of dissuading patients from coming into a particular doctor's office.

"What I want to say, finally, is that we won't be able to bring our kids back if they change their minds five years from now and tell us the HIV virus, or whatever it is that causes AIDS, can be transmitted in the air just like any other virus. I love my daughter, and I'll be damned if I'm willing to take a chance with her life if there's any risk at all. If anyone in this auditorium can prove to me that there isn't a risk, let him or her stand up and do it.''

Thunderous applause broke out for her father's speech, and once again Sarah was conflicted. She was glad he hadn't made an ass of himself, but at the same time, she hoped Dr. Light would meet his challenge and prove to him that he was wrong.

She looked over at David. He was scowling as he whispered something to his father.

There were several more speakers, then Mrs. Willett called on Dr. Light.

''My name is Paul Light, and I've lived in Southern California all of my life and in Longacre most of my life. I even went to UCLA as an undergraduate and as a medical student, and I am presently on the staff at Longacre General Hospital while I continue to do research in AIDS at UCLA.''

As soon as he announced he was doing AIDS research, a murmur went through the audience.

''Mr. Alexander is right about a lot of the things he said,'' Dr. Light went on. ''Researchers do contradict themselves, and they have contradicted themselves about AIDS. However, they do agree on several things. One—AIDS in this country is primarily transmitted by sexual contact. It is also transmitted by blood, and therefore you can get AIDS by sharing a needle with someone who already has the virus, or if tainted blood is transfused into your body. This is why intravenous drug users have contracted the disease and why hemophiliacs have also gotten it. We have better testing methods now, however, and we're working on perfecting those so that people can accept transfusions with less fear of becoming infected.

''Two—the HIV virus is very fragile and cannot live in the air for very long. During sexual contact it is sheltered from the air and therefore has a chance of surviving longer when it is carried in semen and blood. The reason the HIV virus is found only in fifty percent of people with AIDS near death is because the virus, though it has devastated the immune system, is so worn down by the time it has developed into Kaposi's sarcoma or Pneumocystis carinii pneumonia, which actually causes death, the DNA in the cells has changed, and it has disappeared from the system.

"While it is true that you can get AIDS if an infected person's blood is infused with yours, if you take proper precautions, you can treat an AIDS patient with no ill effects even if his or her blood is spilled. Thousands of medical workers have been exposed to AIDS patients. Twelve have been infected, and those twelve admitted that they had not taken the necessary precautions such as wearing masks and rubber gloves.

"In New York more people with AIDS contracted it using tainted needles than by sexual contact. In the Los Angeles area, however, the disease had been primarily transmitted by sexual contact, and this, friends and neighbors, is what we should be concerned about. Not whether Craig Hill can transmit the disease by breathing on our children. We should understand that, whether we like it or not, many of our children are sexually active, and because this disease is transmitted sexually, it is the first disease that strikes strong, healthy people because they are the ones who are usually the most active. When our children go to bed with someone, they also go to bed with anyone that person has slept with in the past eight years. AIDS may have a long latent period, and you can be infected by the most healthy-looking person around.

"Three—AIDS cannot, and I repeat, cannot, be transmitted by casual contact. All researchers agree about this. There must be an exchange of blood or semen. As a medical researcher, as a parent, and as a human being, I beg you to consider what I've said and to make a rational, not an emotional, decision when you decide whether or not to remove Craig Hill from the classroom."

Sarah stood up and clapped when Dr. Light finished his speech. So did several others in the audience, but the majority of people sat silently waiting for the next speaker to appear.

"Sit down," her father hissed at her.

Sarah was shocked. She thought her father would have been convinced by Dr. Light's speech.

She flopped down on her seat and tried to avoid his glare.

By midnight, they were winding down, and Mrs. Willett suggested they call the meeting to a halt saying that most of what had been said in the past hour had been repetitious. Everyone agreed.

"I ask for a call for adjournment, then," she said. "The board will meet in a closed session and make our decision before the end of the holiday vacation. In the meantime, the board agreed beforehand that we think it only fair to remove Mr. Hill from his duties in the classroom until a decision is made."

"Pardon me," Dr. Light said, "but I believe all board meetings must be open to the public."

"That is incorrect," Mrs. Willett said coolly. "We will apprise you all of our decision as soon as we can agree."

The meeting was adjourned, and Sarah left with her parents.

Outside the Civic Center people continued milling around and exchanging information. No one's mind had been changed. When Sarah spotted David and his parents, she began walking over to them, but her father pulled her back sharply, and without saying a word she knew that the lines had been drawn.

Chapter Nineteen

She knew she should get out of bed and help her mother in the kitchen, but she couldn't make herself push off the covers. Getting through Thanksgiving without Doug was difficult, but the thought of spending Christmas without him was impossible.

After David had left last night, she had stood staring at the tree for a long time. There were plenty of presents underneath it. Her parents, knowing how hard this was for her, had overcompensated, which made her angrier at them than she already was. Tensions were high, and the air bristled when they were in the same room together. She could barely talk to her father civilly, and even when she had dropped to the floor to look at the names on each of the gifts and saw that most of them were for her, she was still angry. There was nothing for Doug—except the CD player that was tucked away in the back of her closet. She had skimped on everyone else's gift, including David's, so she could buy something special for Doug—just in case.

She was sure she'd hear from him yesterday. She had refused to leave the house all day because she knew he'd appear like a wise man from the east bearing gifts, and that her father and mother would take him in. They'd have to.

But he hadn't come. And he hadn't called, so instead of anticipating the exhilaration and excitement of Christmas morning around the tree with her family, she was lying in bed trying to decide how she could get out of having dinner with the Collinses, when the phone rang. She picked it up at the same time someone in the kitchen picked up the extension, but she said hello first.

"Sarah?"

"Doug!" she yelled, sitting up in bed, her whole body tensed, ready to spring up and out to meet him wherever he was.

"Hi, kid."

"Where are you?"

"Home," he said with a chuckle.

"Here? You're here?"

"I'm at my house."

"But where—I've been trying to find you forever. Your number was cut—"

She could feel a presence next to her, but she didn't look up to see who it was until it was too late. Her father reached down and yanked the cord out of the wall, and the phone went dead. She leaped out of bed and plunged it into the wall again, but when she held the receiver to her ear, all she heard was a dial tone.

She grabbed her robe and raced into the living room to confront her father. "What'd he do? Tell me. What did he do that was so terrible you won't even let me talk to him?"

"You're better off not knowing."

"And who are you to decide that?"

"Your father."

"That doesn't give you the right to make decisions for me. I've been trying and trying to find him. I call information once a week to see if there's a listing in his name, and now he's finally gotten in touch with me, and what do you do? You throw him out all over again. He's never going to call again. Never."

"Not today, please, Sarah," her father begged.

"Not today. You say that every day. I can't take it anymore. You think you're so smart, smarter than anyone else. You always think you're right about everything. *Everything.* Well, tell me what he did so I can decide for myself whether you're right or wrong, 'cause, guess what, I don't buy everything you have to sell anymore. You can be wrong, just like everyone else. You're wrong about a lot of things, damn it! Whatever he did can't possibly be as bad as what you're doing.''

Her father flew across the room and slapped her face. They both stood there stunned for a moment, then she turned around and ran to the back of the house.

She locked herself in the bathroom, dressed as quickly as she could, and left the house without saying a word to anyone. She knew where she was going as soon as she walked out the door, but she wasn't sure exactly how to get there because this was a holiday, and the buses ran erratically.

Luckily, she had to wait only a half hour, and she boarded the bus feeling a tremendous sense of relief—as well as a knot of sorrow and fear.

As she walked up the path to David's house, he was coming out the front door.

"Sarah—"

"Can I go with you?"

"Sure, but—"

"I need to be with you."

"We were just leaving. You wanna wait here till we get back? We'll only be gone about an hour."

"No. I want to come, too—if it's okay."

"I think it's okay, but you might get a little freaked out. Sure you don't want to wait here?"

"I won't get freaked out."

At that moment the rest of David's family exited the house. Mark, who could have passed for normal if you were expecting a punk rock band, was carrying a huge sack of presents that he threw into the trunk of the car. It looked as if he'd made some concessions for the family. His hair was still dyed, but it was dyed pitch black instead of orange, probably to match the leather jacket David had given him for Christmas, and he was wearing an almost new pair of jeans with only the knees ripped.

"Merry Christmas, Sarah," David's mother said, as she gave her a hug. "I didn't know you were coming with us. How nice."

"If you don't mind," Sarah said.

David's mother and father looked at each other for a moment. His father was obviously torn.

"Do your parents know where we're going?" he asked.

"She's a big girl, dad. She doesn't need her parents' permission," David said intervening for her.

"Of course," Dr. Light said, putting his arm around Sarah.

When they walked into the lobby of the hospital, she held her breath for a moment. It looked like any other lobby at first. Big Christmas tree with presents underneath it, music playing, decorations. Except wheelchairs sat cramped and empty along the walls waiting for their passengers, and the antiseptic smell of the room made her nose tingle.

They took the elevator up and got off at the thirteenth floor. Very appropriate, she thought. As they walked past each empty room, she noticed a sign outside the doors announcing AIDS patients occupied those rooms, and she winced thinking how hard it must be to be reminded of this every time you came in or out of your room.

As they approached a large open area, she saw people milling around. There was a tree here, too, and lots of decorations. Food. One group was singing Christmas carols, and other people were exchanging small talk and information.

Sarah noticed that many of the people seemed to walk with a certain shuffle, as if they were wearing ice skates.

Only they didn't glide along smoothly like skaters; they jerked as if they couldn't control their feet.

She heard snatches of conversation all around her. Most of the patients talked about weight.

"How much did you lose this week?" she heard one woman ask an emaciated man.

"I only lost a quarter of a pound," another man said.

"I'm taking this new medication. It's a miracle. I gained three ounces," a third man said.

Another man, who looked very thin and pale, but who was not wearing a hospital bracelet, was complaining about his last trip to an AIDS clinic somewhere. She didn't catch the name of the clinic. Only that he had waited three hours to see a doctor who was so overcommitted he had only three minutes to spend with him.

She felt weak, her knees turned to rubber, and she grabbed David's arm. Lying in a hospital bed nearby was a man gradually turning into a skeleton. She could see his bones under the bluish skin, and she almost gasped when she looked into the hollows of his sunken, empty eyes.

She looked away and saw other patients huddled in corners by themselves, talking to no one. Perhaps they were afraid of learning anything more about their own mortality.

"Look at that," David said, nodding toward the other side of the room. Mark was gently helping one of the patients out of bed.

While they were watching Mark, a handsome young man, wearing glasses much too large for his face, came dashing across the room. He threw his arms around David and gave him a bear hug. "Didn't think you were going to make it, gorgeous," he said to David.

David laughed and hugged the man back. "Wouldn't miss this for anything. Where else could I come to see the latest men's fashions?"

"Like my new sweater?" the man said, preening.

Sarah smiled at the young man. He was pale, but certainly didn't look any sicker than a lot of people walking around in the outside world. She knew he was a patient, however, because he wore a hospital bracelet around his wrist.

"Glad you finally got one that fits," David said.

"My new diet," the man said. "Didn't you just hate the way everything hung on me? I swear, I think someone's missing the chance to make a lot of bucks. Every other diet plan has ultimately failed. AIDS is foolproof. What do you say? Think we ought to market it?"

"You've always got a scheme, Jake," David said, laughing. "This is Sarah. Sarah—Jake."

"Oh, so this is the girl you've been talking about," Jake said, smiling at Sarah with the whitest teeth she'd ever seen.

"No, she's the other one," David said laughing.

"Well, I like this one better. If I were hetero," he said, "she'd sure be my type."

"And if I weren't, you'd be my type," David laughed, "but—"

"Yeah, that's what you always say. You know where I met this weird bird?" Jake asked Sarah, interrupting David.

She shook her head no.

"In the waiting room of his father's office. I mean, how was I to know he was straight?"

Sarah was shocked at the way Jake and David were kidding around. Shocked for lots of reasons. But she also understood this was the way they related to each other, and it was okay.

"I didn't know your father saw patients," Sarah said. "I thought he did research."

"He does," David said, "but he sees patients when he makes rounds with the residents at the hospital."

"But not in an office?"

"Not in an office."

"But—"

Both David and Jake started to laugh again. "Jake is a third-year resident."

"A doctor?" Sarah asked, shocked once again.

"Was—a resident—that is," Jake said. "I'm still a doctor. Guess that can't be taken away from me."

"They won't let you practice anymore?"

"Not a question of 'let,' " he said with a sigh. "More a question of can't. The villain's not the hospital. The villain's the damn disease. It's stolen everything. My energy. My friends. My parents. My peace of mind. My life," he said softly.

"My dad says Jake's one of the best residents he's ever trained," David said quickly. Then all of them fell silent for a moment, though Sarah knew they were all thinking the exact same thing. The training would never do anyone any good.

"Yeah, your dad's okay," Jake said, trying to sound cheerful again. "Of course, he's not as sexy as you are, but I'm fond of the old guy anyway."

"I don't think he'd love being called an old guy," David said. "Especially since he thinks he's pretty sexy, even if you don't."

"Well, I'll give him a closer look the next time I see him," Jake said, a little strained—as if someone were emptying his tank of energy, and he was running out of gas.

"So when you coming for dinner?" David asked. "My mom misses you."

Before Jake could answer, David turned to Sarah and explained, "My dad brought this joker home to dinner three years ago, and my mom adopted him. We haven't been able to get rid of him since."

"David," Sarah said, nudging him. This fooling around was getting out of hand.

"Hey," Jake said, punching David's arm lightly. "At the rate I'm losing weight, you'll be rid of me in no time."

"I'm sorry," David said, stumbling over his words. "I didn't mean, I was only trying—"

"Don't. That's what I like about you. About your family.

No one pretends the grim reaper ain't right around the corner, just waiting for me to give up. If it weren't for your macabre sense of humor to egg me on, I'd probably have reached for that scythe a long time ago."

"Chase him away, buddy. We're not ready to lose you yet. When you getting out of this place?"

"Big day's tomorrow."

"Then you come to dinner on Tuesday or Wednesday."

"Yeah. Sure," Jake said with a sigh. "I'll give you a call. Let you know if I can make it."

He patted David on the arm again, but David didn't let him just walk away. He gave Jake a hug, holding him for that extra second longer than he had to—just to let him know.

"Hope I see you again, Sarah," Jake said. "And I do mean that in all sincerity."

"Yeah, me too," she said watching him slowly shuffle off toward another group of people.

When he reached the group, Jake sat down wearily, and someone leaned over to him, then separated himself from the rest of the group, giving Sarah a clear view of a young man who had been obscured from her vision before.

"Doug," she whispered.

"What?"

"Doug," she repeated, still staring at him across the room. "My brother's over there," she mumbled to David as she grabbed his arm without taking her eyes off Doug.

Chapter Twenty

She sat in the backseat of Doug's car staring at the familiar slope of his shoulders and the unfamiliar shaft of Terry's ponytail. She was glad Terry was with them so she would have a chance to think. She had wanted to see Doug so badly. She had looked for him everywhere she went, at the movies, in stores, along the beach, but she had found him when she least expected to, and now she didn't know what to say to him. She suddenly felt shy and embarrassed, as if he were a stranger, not her own brother.

David's family, knowing she wanted to spend time with Doug, quietly said their good-byes and slipped out of the hospital. David said he'd call her later, though they were both so confused and rushed, she wondered as she sat in the car just where she would be later.

When they pulled up in front of a building in the middle of factories and industrial plants in what she thought was probably downtown L.A., Terry jumped out of the car, said he was glad to have finally met her, and excused himself. He was off to see a friend at a nearby café.

Sarah followed Doug to a service elevator in a building that looked as if it were some kind of warehouse. They got out and were immediately inside of a large space that had been carefully decorated with a lot of charm, if not money.

The secondhand furniture had been covered with a pink-ish canvas material, and a coffee table, once the end of a spool of wire, had been stained and rested on a wooden block in front of the couch. Whimsical prints by Miró hung on the walls.

"And this is our room with a view," Doug said, leading her over to a bank of windows overlooking the seediest part of town. For a moment, she was anxious about Doug's living here, then she realized how proud he was to be show-ing off his own place, so she just smiled and said it was great.

"Can I get you anything?" he asked formally. "A soft drink, or something?"

"No, thanks," she answered, just as formally. "I'd like to use the bathroom, though."

"Over there," he said, pointing to a door at the back of the loft that provided the opening to a makeshift bath-room.

On her way there, she looked into an alcove that housed a queen-sized bed covered with a bright Marimekko com-forter. On the wall behind the bed were matching sheets that hung loosely, making a colorful, extended headboard.

What a neat idea, she thought as she walked into the bathroom, smiling at Doug and Terry's imagination. Then she stopped cold in her tracks and broke out into a sweat. There was something wrong.

When she came out of the bathroom, she quickly walked past the alcove without looking at it, though she couldn't get the image of the big bed out of her mind.

She coughed twice to announce her return since Doug's back was to her. He was busy putting a tape into a tape deck—not nearly as good as the CD player she had bought him for Christmas, she thought proudly, and she wished she could, by some miracle, transport it from her closet to this room.

"So I guess you know," he said without turning around to face her.

"Is that what he's been hiding from me all these months?"

"He didn't tell you?"

"No."

"You must have suspected."

"No," she said, though she wasn't sure if that was true or not. She scanned her brain. Maybe somewhere back, way back, she had had some kind of inkling, but the thought had never crossed the gap from unconscious to conscious. She had never let it.

"I'm surprised," he said as he turned to look at her.

"Why did he have to know? Why'd you have to tell him?"

"Couldn't live with the lies anymore. Didn't want to, I guess."

"But why—"

" 'Cause that's the way it is. It's always been that way."

"Even in Ohio?"

"Even in Ohio, believe it or not."

"He can't talk about it."

"I thought he'd come around eventually."

"Maybe he will. I don't know."

"He saw us in the car. Me and Terry."

"You wanted him to," she said, a little angry that he had, in a sense, taken the coward's way out."

"Yeah. I guess I did. I just didn't know how to tell him. I tried, but he wouldn't listen."

"That's not one of his strong points—listening."

"Tell me about it."

There was a long, awkward pause.

"I missed you a lot."

"I missed you, too. After I tried calling you, and you

didn't return my call, I was devastated, afraid if I tried to get in touch—"

"But your number was cut—"

"I know. I know," he said, shaking his head sadly. "But I never thought of that."

"All this time," she said. "I looked all over for you."

"Bet you didn't look down here," he said, and he laughed at himself, the way he used to, so everything would be all right. "How's mom?" he asked, looking at her for some clue.

"She's okay. Still like the scarecrow in *The Wizard of Oz*. Doesn't have a brain in her head."

"She's not so dumb."

"Maybe not, but she sure doesn't have a mind of her own."

"You're too hard on her."

"She misses you. I hear her crying sometimes."

"Does it bother you?"

"You mean—about you?"

"Yeah."

"I don't know. Maybe a little, but not 'cause it makes a difference to me. 'Cause it must be hard for you. I don't know. I guess it doesn't bother me personally," she said, her voice trailing off into a squeak.

"I'm the same person I always was."

"I know. I'm not the same person I always was, though."

"I see that. You've really grown up in the past few months."

"Not enough."

"Meaning?"

"I had my own little confrontation with dad this morning, which felt kind of good at the moment, but now I'm scared. I'm afraid he'll pack up my things and park them in front of the house like he did yours."

"He wouldn't do that to you."

"Not today, maybe," she said without a touch of irony. "The Collinses are there for Christmas dinner."

"The Collinses," Doug roared. "One good reason not to go home again."

"Wouldn't they just die if they knew?" Sarah asked, feeling a little giddy. "Emily and Wendy."

"What a bitch."

"Which one?"

"Both of them."

"Oh god, aren't they horrible?" Sarah said, laughing.

"At least if she knew, maybe Wendy would stop trying to corner me every time we happen to be in the same room."

They both laughed at the image of Wendy following Doug as he walked from room to room trying to shake her. She was like a leech. Once she got hold of you, she wouldn't let go.

"You could stay here with us," Doug said, still laughing.

"Great," Sarah said. "Just what you need."

"I mean it. Terry wouldn't mind. We'd be a family."

"Some family."

"That's what we both miss most, I guess. Family."

"I'm sorry, Doug. I didn't mean to make fun of what you said. We'd be a good family. The three of us."

"In case," he said. "Just in case you need us."

"Thanks. I mean it."

"So do I."

"Doug," she said slowly, "I have to ask you something," she continued, wanting to ask him what had been on her mind since she came back into the living room area. "Doug—I mean, you don't have to tell me if you don't want to, but—yeah—you do have to tell me, 'cause I need to know. What were you doing there today? Why were you at the hospital? Do *you* . . . ?" She couldn't say it. She saw an image of the man who was evolving into a skeleton, and she couldn't make herself say it.

"No—No. That's not it," he said, reassuring her. "I'm

a volunteer. When the first friend I met here died of AIDS in August, I decided to become a volunteer for the AIDS Project L.A. That's where I met Terry. In the training program.''

"Training program to be a volunteer?''

"Three months,'' he said.

"You're willing to give up all that time for them?''

"For us,'' Doug said softly. "All of us.''

"Aren't you scared?''

"That I'll get it? No. That I won't be able to take the psychological pressure of holding a dying man in my arms? Yes. I'm afraid of that, but I think I'll be able to do it if I have to.''

"I'm scared for you—of the other thing.''

"Terry and I are monogamous—like an old married couple—and we've both been tested several times. Making love is great, but it ain't worth dying for. We're cautious. Very cautious.''

"Doug—I just wish—''

"Hey, you're not immune either, kid. Just cause you're squeaky clean and as straight as they come doesn't mean the guy you were with today is. If you know what I mean.''

"We haven't—''

"But some day you might. If not with him, then with another guy you fall in love with, and you'll know he loves you, too, if he uses a condom. If he won't, ax the guy. It isn't worth it,'' he said, sounding more like a father than an older brother. She had never been so intimate with anyone before, not even David. Hell, she'd never had such an extended conversation with her brother before today. She suddenly realized she not only missed him, she loved him. For the first time that she could remember she went over to him, put her arms around him, and hugged him as hard as she could.

"So, what do you say?'' he asked, hugging her back. "Want to call and see if it's okay to go home, or should we just drive past and see if the clothes are outside?''

Chapter Twenty-one

Doug drove her home and let her off in front of the house. He waited until he was sure everything was all right, then she heard him drive away, taking a small part of her with him. But, at least now, she knew where he was, and if she needed him, or if she just wanted to be with him, she knew how to get in touch.

She walked into the house gingerly. Her father was sitting in the living room watching TV, and her mother was in the kitchen cleaning up. The house still had the feel of a place not quite put back together again after being invaded by the outside world.

She didn't say anything because she wasn't quite sure what her attitude should be. She wasn't angry anymore, because the main reason for her anger had dissipated. And though she was upset with her father because of his unenlightened attitude and with her mother for backing up his hysteria, Sarah knew she had also been wrong for not understanding their pain as well as their anger. She may not have deserved a slap in the face, but she didn't deserve a medal of honor either. So she stood there waiting to see what they would do.

They didn't do anything. Without lifting his eyes from the TV, her father mumbled a hello, and when her mother called, "What?" from the kitchen, he merely replied, "Sarah's home."

"That's good," her mother said as she continued rinsing the dishes.

In a sense, it was a relief. She'd had enough in the way of confrontations and surprises for one day, and all she wanted to do was fall into bed and sleep for about a month.

"How was dinner?" she asked quietly.

"Fine. It was fine," her father said.

"Need any help?" she asked her mother as she walked past the kitchen.

"No thanks," her mother said.

"I guess I'll go to bed, then. I'm beat."

"Good night."

"Night."

She washed her face, brushed her teeth, and fell into an exhausted sleep that knocked her out for twelve hours. The only reason she woke up was because the phone rang, and she thought it was her alarm.

She reached for it automatically, though technically she was not really awake, and groaned into the mouthpiece.

"Sorry," David apologized. "Didn't mean to wake you up, but I couldn't wait any longer."

"Wait for what?" she asked, still groggy.

"To find out what happened."

"What do you mean?"

"With you and Doug."

"Oh, yeah," she said, trying to clear her head and convince herself it hadn't been a dream.

"So did you find out what he did?"

"He works in some computer place and goes to school part time."

"I mean what he did that made your father so uptight."

"Not really. I mean I don't know exactly what happened, but I know why my dad won't let him live here."

"Okay. I'll bite. Why?" David asked, annoyed that she wasn't more forthcoming and that he had to all but pry the information out of her.

"David—I'm still half-asleep. Could I call you back or something?"

"Fine."

"It's just that I don't want to talk about it over the phone, is all."

"I said, fine."

"Don't get mad."

"Okay. I won't get mad. When can I come over? We have to talk about what we're doing New Year's Eve."

"Give me an hour."

"See you."

"See you."

She got dressed and walked into the kitchen to make some breakfast. The kitchen looked as if her mother had been up half the night getting to places that hadn't been touched in months. She'd never seen it so clean.

"Mom?" she called tentatively.

No one answered.

"Mom?" she called more loudly.

Still no answer.

She must have gone out, Sarah thought, and her father had obviously left for work hours ago. Good, 'cause she still didn't know how she was supposed to act around them, or even how she wanted to act.

By the time she finished piddling around, David was ringing the doorbell. When she went to answer it, she found her mother's note taped to the inside of the front door. "Emily and I went to return Christmas presents. Be back around five." She'd have to get David out of there before then, or her parents would throw a fit. To avoid conflict, she and David usually went to his house when they wanted some privacy, because her parents still didn't trust her enough to let her have kids over if one of them wasn't home. That, of course, was one of the things about them that drove her insane. It was so hypocritical. She knew, and they knew, and she knew they knew, and they knew she knew that if she wanted to do drugs or have sex, she could find any number of places to do it. It didn't make any difference if she was at home or not, but that was the rule, and it was easier to follow it than to argue about it anymore.

After she explained to David what had happened the day before, and after she had answered most of his questions, some of which were unanswerable, they talked about other things. About how complicated it was growing up and having to make your own decisions. About how painful it was to recognize that your values might be different from your parents' values. About how wonderful it is to feel free enough to be who you are and how scary it is to try and find out exactly who that you is.

"It's so much easier when you're a kid," Sarah said. "You do things because your parents tell you to, and even if you don't agree with them, you don't really think you have a choice. You can throw a fit if you want to, or you can steal your mom's lipstick and hope you won't get caught, but you still feel wrong doing it. Even when you think they're wrong, you think you're more wrong. They put all this guilt out there so when you do something, you always have to think, 'They're going to be so embarrassed. They're going to be so upset.' "

"Me and my dad talked a lot about that," David said. "He thinks that's one of the reasons Mark acts so crazy. 'Cause he and my mom were always saying things like, 'You have to think about other people. You can't just go through life doing what you want to do. There are people who need help,' and stuff like that. But what they didn't recognize—till it was almost too late—was that Mark needed help, too. Only he felt guilty asking for any attention when he thought there were so many people who 'really' needed it. Know what I mean?"

"Sort of. You mean Mark made himself sick so he wouldn't feel guilty about your parents spending time with him instead of with people who need help."

"Yeah. That's why he started doing drugs, and dyeing his hair crazy colors, and stuff."

"God, if *your* parents make mistakes—"

"Everybody makes mistakes."

"Yeah, I guess they do."

"So, in order to avoid making another one—let's clear up a very important matter. New Year's Eve."

"A very important matter."

"What do you want to do?"

"I don't know. What do you?"

"My parents are having a bunch of people over."

"Do we have to? I mean, not that I don't like your parents, but I won't know any of those people."

"Okay. That's ruled out."

"My brother's having a few of his friends over."

"Neither one of us knows them."

"Out."

"Bobby called me this morning and invited us to an open house—"

"Bobby!"

"Out."

"Guess we'll just have to go to a movie and fool around."

"We don't have to go to a movie to do that," he said, moving closer to her.

"I know," she said catching her breath.

"Who's home?"

"No one."

"When will they be?"

"Four-thirty."

"We have three and a half hours."

"I'm nervous."

"So am I."

"I've never done it before."

"I'm not exactly an expert."

They were so close a sheet of paper couldn't have passed between them.

"There are too many windows in here. Where's your room?"

She took his hand and led him down the hallway.

"I don't want to push you," he mumbled as he kissed her.

"I wouldn't do it if I didn't love you," she whispered. Then she realized she had said the "L" word, and she froze.

"I love you, too," he whispered in her ear as he unbuttoned her blouse.

So this was it, she thought. In one sense she was ready, and in another, well, she was scared she wouldn't know what to do. It might be the most natural thing in the world, but no book could substitute for the real experience. All the "what if's" went surging through her brain at the same moment, and just when she remembered what Doug had said, and just when she was about to panic, David reached into his back pocket and took out a condom.

And she knew he loved her.

Chapter Twenty-two

The rest of the vacation passed in a haze of euphoria and goodwill toward everyone. Sarah and David even stopped at the Collinses' New Year's day to say hello and wish everyone a happy New Year, which she meant sincerely.

Now that she was an adult, Sarah saw the world a bit differently, less critically. While it was true that Emily Collins was a gossip and a social climber, she was also good-hearted and open. And while Wendy had totally different values from hers and was a complete burnout, she also understood that a little better, too. Being shifted around from parent to parent might have its good points, but it also made for some heavy-duty insecurity. No wonder Wendy idolized the only thing that gave her any sense of permanence—boutiques and department stores.

She also understood her parents better. It wasn't that she accepted the things they said or did, but that she accepted them and knew that just because they were the way they were, didn't mean she had to be. She suddenly understood the pressures on both her parents. Her father had had to show the main office he could make a go of it in California. Her mother had been plopped down in the middle of a foreign place, too, and it must have been just as hard for her to give up her friends in Ohio and inch her way in here as it had been for Sarah.

They still made no mention of Doug, and she just let it go, preferring to talk to him when they weren't around. She was so happy to know where he was and how to get in touch with him that she managed, somehow, to speak with him every day.

As far as their attitude toward David was concerned—they couldn't help but like him. All adults liked him because he was so grown up. But when her father tried to talk to him about Mr. Hill, she could see the tension rising, and she always interrupted, saying they had to go, or some such thing. This was still a sore issue with her father, one that would be resolved at the board meeting tonight. Her father was sure Mrs. Willett and the rest of the board would agree with him and that Craig Hill would be out of the school forever.

They had had a sub Monday and Tuesday, and now they all sat in the packed auditorium waiting for the board members to appear.

To their surprise Craig Hill walked in also, just as Mrs. Willett was calling the meeting to order.

"We have called this special meeting once again, this time, I hope, to resolve the issue of Craig Hill's continued appointment at Longacre High," Mrs. Willett said. "We have spent many, many long hours among ourselves trying to come up with the best possible solution for all of us," she continued.

Sarah sunk down in her seat. It sounded as if they were going to push Mr. Hill out of the classroom and into some desk job away from the students.

"We, on the board, know this is an emotional issue—a sensitive one—so we hope that once our decision is announced, you will all go along with us and accept our judgment because we are your elected representatives. We have tried, not only to consider your various points of view, but to also learn as much as we could about the matter ourselves. We have also asked Mr. Hill if he would join us at

the meeting this evening so he could hear firsthand exactly
what our position is and why we have taken it.''

Sarah looked around the room. Everyone was sitting on
the edge of his or her chair, craning necks to locate Mr.
Hill, whom she had seen take a seat in the fifth or sixth row
on the side of the auditorium.

David was sitting several rows in front of her with his
parents. She had wanted to sit with them, too, as a show of
her support for their ideas, but, at the last minute, she had
changed her mind.

''What we had here was an unprecedented situation,''
Mrs. Willett said, ''so we moved carefully and cautiously,
with regard to legal matters as well as scholastic ones, and
our lawyer, who has studied the material at hand, agrees
with our conclusion.''

''What is it, already,'' a man shouted from the audience.

''I don't mean to prolong this,'' Mrs. Willett said. ''I
guess I'm just a bit nervous about your accepting our decision, and I think it's important for all of us concerned that
you understand how and why we made it.''

''First of all, we have no reason to believe that Craig Hill
has ever made any sexual overtures to any member of our
student body. If he had that would be reason enough to
bring charges against him or any other teacher, homosexual
or heterosexual, but he has, as far as the administration is
concerned, been an exemplary teacher in every way.''

''Second, since he has had no intimate contact with any
student at Longacre, as far as we know, and we do not think
there is any reason to believe that might happen in the
future, we feel there is no chance of his transmitting the
disease—AIDS—to anyone at the school—faculty or students.''

A roar of applause went up from the audience. Against
the roar were groans and shouts of disapproval, but Sarah
smiled from ear to ear. She knew Mr. Hill had won.

Her father got up angrily and stormed out of the auditorium, her mother, the Collinses, and a dozen other people following him, but Sarah sat tight, her hands sore from clapping.

Mrs. Willett banged the gavel again and again, calling for order, but no one wanted to be still. Finally, above the din, she shouted into the mike, "If you'll just give me two more minutes of your time, we can all go out and celebrate."

Another roar of applause went up from the crowd. Other dissenters walked out and slammed the doors at the back of the auditorium, then finally the noise simmered down.

"Thank you. Thank you," Mrs. Willett said. "It wasn't an easy decision, believe me, but I think that most of us are together on this. What we've learned, probably the most important thing we've learned from all of this, is that while AIDS can't be transferred by casual contact, it can be transferred sexually, which means that our children are, in a very real way, at risk. Not from Mr. Hill, but from one another. Ignorance will kill our children. Not Craig Hill. They must learn that if they do have sex—"

At this point a group of parents booed Mrs. Willett down, shouting, "No sex education in our school!"

"Just a minute. Just a minute, please," Mrs. Willett begged the audience. "We can close our eyes to this if we want to. We can go on pretending it's not going to affect us, that our kids don't have sex, but the reality is that one third of the girls and one half of the boys in our nation's high schools have had sexual intercourse, beginning on the average at age sixteen."

"What are you trying to do up there," a woman shouted, "tell our kids it's okay? Everyone else does it, so they can, too?"

Another member of the board asked Mrs. Willett if he could speak for a moment, and she relinquished the floor to him.

"We're not trying to justify premarital sex," Mr. Conklin said. "In fact, in our home, at our church, we're very much against it. Our children know how we feel, how our church feels, but that doesn't mean it's going to stop them. I hope it will, but sticking my head in the sand and praying it won't happen isn't the way to go.

"Frankly, I'm alarmed by the new data we're faced with that indicates that we're ripe for an epidemic among teenagers. The Centers for Disease Control in Atlanta says there are four hundred and fifteen cases of AIDS among kids from ages thirteen to nineteen. That's a forty percent increase in the last two years. And that's for *reported* cases. New studies indicate that infection rate in some teenage groups is higher than that for adults."

"Let's face it. Many teenagers have multiple partners, and very few of them use condoms. Education doesn't force kids to have sex. But lack of education might cause them to pay for it with their lives if they do. Kids don't think about the future. We have to."

"The Center for Population Options also estimates that about two hundred thousand teens have used IV drugs," another man on the board interjected over the roar of the crowd, which hadn't calmed down yet.

"We don't have that problem at Longacre," another parent shouted.

"Order," Mrs. Willett shouted, banging the gavel. "The meeting will please come to order. If you raise your hands, you will be recognized." She pointed to a man in the far corner of the auditorium. He got up and walked to the podium.

"My name is Guy Turner. My daughter went to school in Longacre from prekindergarten till last year. Last year she dropped out of high school. Well, that's not exactly true," he sighed. "She flunked out. She's an intravenous drug user. Right now there's not much we can do about it, either, except make sure she uses clean needles. You see, she's an addict. She's had therapy. She's been in drug rehab centers three times. She's been clean for two or three weeks at a time, but then . . ." his voice trailed off. "Then it starts all over again. But you know what? You know what my greatest fear is—not that she continues using, but that she will die from sharing a needle with someone who has AIDS. And the only way I can help her is to try to get to her in some way, teach her not to use dirty needles. Not to share needles with anyone, including the six or seven other kids from Longacre she uses with."

He looked into the audience. "Some of them are your kids. And some of them belong to a few of you who have been yelling about not teaching prevention in our schools."

He walked to his seat and there was a hush in the auditorium.

"Thank you, Mr. Turner," Mrs. Willett said finally. "Thank you. I know how difficult that was. What I want to add before we adjourn this meeting, if there are no other comments, is that our recommendation is that the school create an AIDS awareness program, mandatory for every student at Longacre, and we hope this program will be a guiding light for all the other communities in our country."

Again, there was applause, and Sarah was so proud and so happy to be a part of this revolutionary process, this look at democracy in action.

From the back of the room came one more shout, however. "Wait. Wait. You guys didn't recognize me," Bobby shouted as he ran to the front of the auditorium.

"My apologies, Mr. . . . ?" Mrs. Willett said.

"Muladore. The name's Bobby Muladore, and I just wanted to add my say-so, too. See, I think there's this one other little thing you guys forgot to say in all this talk, and that is that Hill is, in my opinion, the greatest teacher at the school. Actually, not just the greatest—the only *good* teacher. Okay? Okay, so I said it, and I'm glad," Bobby muttered, suddenly embarrassed by all the cheers.

"If there's nothing else then, the board would like to publicly apologize to Craig Hill for any embarrassment this incident might have caused him and to let him know we value his services and hope he will go back to the classroom tomorrow with the same enthusiasm for his work he's shown in the past.''

Sarah jumped to her feet and hugged the person now sitting next to her, though she had no idea who that person was.

Chapter Twenty-three

Sarah and David sat on the floor of Doug and Terry's apartment, a bottle of champagne and four glasses spread out in front of them.

"You did it," Sarah said proudly.

"We're gonna miss you around here next year," Doug said. "Rhode Island is on the other side of the world."

"Of the country, at least," Terry said as he popped the cork very professionally, without spilling a drop of the precious wine.

"Excellent," David said.

"I haven't been a waiter for three years for nothing," Terry said as he poured each of them a glass.

"So when are you going to hear from Ohio State?" Doug asked Sarah.

She didn't answer him for a moment. Then without looking directly at anyone, she said, "Most of the schools send out their acceptances or regrets the middle of April."

"How come you heard now, Dave?" Terry asked.

"Geniuses apply early action," Sarah said, reaching over to give David a hug.

"Come on," he said, blushing. "My father and grandfather went to Brown. They could hardly turn me down."

"Sure," she said. "Just pretend you don't have over a

four point average, and pretend you don't play on the varsity baseball team, and pretend you don't write for the newspaper.''

"Okay. So that all helped," David admitted.

"So a toast," Doug said, raising his glass.

They all did the same, and Sarah felt proud of David, and proud of Doug for getting himself together without any help from their parents, and for being compassionate enough to support other people who needed help. She felt proud of Terry because he stuck by her brother and obviously loved him. And she felt proud of herself for following her own instincts, for promising herself she would try not to sabotage herself in the future, for being able to listen to her parents without blowing up, for understanding them instead of judging them.

It wasn't easy reevaluating. They had come to California intact. A real old-fashioned, all-American family. White, Protestant, middle-class. Two parents, two children—a boy and a girl. Father successful, but not the president of a corporation. Mother a housewife. Nothing in their lives had prepared Sarah for what had happened in the past year.

Their family was now down to three, and in September she would leave, too, coming home only for holidays, and maybe not even then since she was planning on going far away. Not exactly intentionally, but it was about as far away as you could get and still be in the United States.

She was sorry her parents still wouldn't accept Doug and still refused to see him, but that didn't stop her from seeing him, and that didn't stop her from feeling closer to him than she had ever felt before.

And when her father had tried to force her to drop Mr. Hill's class second semester, she had refused to do that, too. She didn't really argue with them about it. She simply said, very quietly and calmly, "There's no evidence that I could possibly catch AIDS from Mr. Hill. I'm sorry you're upset about it, but this class is very important to me, and I'm not going to drop it.''

She had expected her father to hit the ceiling, to lock her door and force her to stay in the house until she changed her mind, but he had just looked at her as if he were seeing someone else. Then he had said, ''As long as you're living in my house, you'll do as I say, and I say you will drop that class. Now.''

She had walked into her room and slammed the door. Then she had begun to pack her clothes and her books. Five minutes later she heard a knock. She froze.

''Can I come in?'' her mother asked.

''Yeah,'' she said so softly, she wasn't sure her mother could even hear her.

''I don't agree with what you're doing,'' her mother had said, ''but—''

''You might as well stop right now,'' Sarah said. ''I'm moving in with Doug and Terry.''

''Please, just listen, Sarah. I know there have been a lot of changes in your life—''

''A lot.''

''And it hasn't been easy, this move.''

''Maybe it's been for the best,'' Sarah said as she continued to pack.

''I don't want you to leave. I don't think I could stand that,'' her mother said quietly. ''I know I'll have to give you up in September, but I'm not ready to let you go yet, and in spite of the fact that you've grown up so much,'' her mother said with tears in her eyes, ''I don't think you want to go, either. You're still my little girl.''

Sarah tried to steel herself against her mother's tears. She was not going to give in. She turned around and threw a pair of tennis shoes into a small duffel bag. Then without warning, huge tears rolled out of her own eyes.

''I'm like an in-between,'' she said as she leaned her

head on her mother's shoulder. "I feel like a grown-up in so many ways, but I'm still just a kid in other ways."

So, she had stayed at home. And she hadn't dropped the art class. She kept a small bag packed, just in case, but her father never mentioned Craig Hill again.

"Did you apply anyplace except Ohio State?" Terry asked Sarah, interrupting her thoughts.

"I didn't apply to Ohio State," she said.

They all turned to look at her.

"But I thought—" Doug said.

"Things change," she said. "We change."

"So where?" David asked.

"Lots of places. The UC system—UC San Diego, maybe. Pratt Institute of Design—"

"An art school?" Doug asked.

"I'm going more and more in that direction," Sarah said. "That's what I want to do with my life."

"Whoa," David said jumping up with excitement. "Rhode Island School of Design is right across the street from Brown."

"That so?" Sarah said, laughing.

"It's a fabulous school. It's great," David said. "You have to apply."

"No, I don't," she said.

"What do you mean. We'd be right next door to each other," David said, confused by her intransigence.

"I know."

"So, I don't understand. Why don't you apply?"

"I already did. Mr. Hill gave me all the information last fall. I had it around for a while, never looked at it because I was so sure I was going to Ohio State, but I got it out recently, and—"

David picked her up off the floor and swung her around the room. "This is fabulous."

"You really want me to be that close to you?" she asked, giggling.

"Are you kidding?" he said.

"I'm not kidding. Mr. Hill talked to the admissions people. They want me."

"Are you kidding? Is she kidding? This is great. This is more than great. It's fabulous."

"Yeah," she said when he put her back on the ground again. "I guess it is, isn't it?"

About the Author

Marilyn Levy, a former English teacher, is currently writing television scripts as well as novels. She is married, has two daughters, and lives in Santa Monica, California.

Teens

learn to make tough choices and the meaning of responsibility in novels by **Marilyn Levy**